DELROY IS HERE

Rhodri Jones
DELROY IS HERE

Unwin Hyman

Published in 1987 by
UNWIN HYMAN LIMITED
15/17 Broadwick Street
London W1V 1FP

© Rhodri Jones 1983
Educational first edition published by
University Tutorial Press in 1983
Reprinted by Unwin Hyman Limited 1987

ISBN 0 7135 2838 9

Printed in Great Britain by
Billing and Sons Ltd, Worcester

ONE

It was letters from school that really worried him. Whenever he got into trouble, the school would write a letter about it to tell his parents.

Delroy Ellis got into trouble a lot. He admitted that. And he was punished for it. He didn't like being punished, but he put up with it. He usually made a big fuss about it, but in the end he normally did what he was told. There was no way of escaping it. So why did they have to send letters as well? Why did they have to let his parents know? They always created hell when they got a letter. That made it a double punishment — first from school, and then from them. It wasn't right.

These thoughts were rumbling through Delroy's mind as he sat in registration at the beginning of school that day. Mrs Lasky, his form teacher, had called the register. Now she was going on about homework and how vital it was. Delroy had heard it all before. The teachers couldn't cover all the work necessary in class time, Mrs Lasky was saying. Pupils had to learn how to study on their own. No one could pass exams without doing revision and extra work out of school.

It was the same old stuff. Delroy supposed that Mrs Lasky knew what she was talking about. But that sort of thing wasn't important to him. He let her words flow over him. He had more urgent matters to think about.

There was that business with Mr Frobisher the day before. It was exactly the kind of thing they would write to his parents about. If they did, Delroy knew precisely what would happen. There would be rows. His father would raise the roof. Life wouldn't be worth living.

Delroy was sure Mr Frobisher wouldn't just let the incident go. He was a stickler for the rules. He always stood on his dignity. If anything was done to offend him, he was certain to report it. Delroy knew this from experience. He had been in trouble with Mr Frobisher before.

Any minute now, Delroy expected Mrs Lasky to call

1

him out and demand an explanation. She had finished nagging about homework. The best thing was not to attract her attention. He kept his eyes down, pretending to check a maths problem in his exercise book. When he next looked up, Mrs Lasky was talking to a group of boys at the back of the room.

Apart from greeting him pleasantly when he had arrived, his form teacher had shown no special interest in Delroy. Perhaps it was going to be all right after all. Perhaps Mr Frobisher had forgotten, or hadn't considered it worth reporting. There was hope yet.

Delroy began to relax. His old exuberance started to bubble up inside him. By the end of registration he was his usual lively self again.

As soon as the bell went he was out of the door and racing down the corridor to his first lesson of the day. He burst into the room. The teacher was still taking his class.

'Sorry, sir,' said Delroy apologetically to the startled face of the teacher. 'I thought the room was empty.'

He closed the door. A huge smile spread across his brown face as he doubled up with delighted laughter. He clicked his fingers repeatedly in the air in self-congratulation. He had known perfectly well that there was a class inside. He enjoyed doing things like that.

Eventually, the teacher let his class go. The pupils charged out of the classroom as though someone had just announced that there was a free issue of sweets from the tuck-shop. Delroy bulldozed his way in, shoving against the tide.

'Hey, that's my foot!' somebody yelled.

Delroy ignored him. He made for his usual seat next to the radiator and the window. He would be comfortable there—especially if there was a football match in the yard outside for him to watch.

But Paul, one of his friends, was already sitting in his place. He hadn't had to change classrooms.

'Out!' commanded Delroy. 'That's my seat.'

'Who says?' asked Paul.

'I says,' replied Delroy aggressively.

Paul may have been one of Delroy's friends, but that

2

didn't give him the right to sit in his seat.

'You ain't my mother, you know,' said Paul calmly.

Delroy grabbed Paul by the shoulder of his blazer and began to pull him bodily from his chair.

'Stop that at once,' ordered Mr Andrews, who had just arrived.

'He's in my seat,' protested Delroy. He turned back to Paul. 'Get out of my seat. You're dead if you don't.'

'I didn't know you had a reserved seat,' said Mr Andrews. 'If the seats belong to anyone, they belong to me, so you'll sit where I tell you to.'

Delroy scowled angrily at Paul. 'Man, you're dead,' he muttered.

'Oh, all right,' said Paul, deciding not to make an issue of it. 'Have your stinking seat.'

He stood up and knocked the chair back. He picked up his books and went to sit at another desk at the front of the class. By this time, another row had broken out on the other side of the room, and this was taking up Mr Andrews' attention. Delroy was able to secure his seat without any further fuss.

''E's t'iefed my pen,' a boy was accusing.

'No I ain't. You callin' me a t'ief?' came the reply.

Suddenly Mr Andrews let out an almighty roar. 'Will you stop that?'

Delroy joined the other pupils in a stunned silence.

'I want you all sitting at your desks,' Mr Andrews went on, loudly and dangerously. 'I want you all to have your books open. Or else you'll be back at the end of school. You Fourth Year boys are always the same.'

There were a few groans, mutters and shufflings as boys found their places. Then a sullen kind of order settled on the room. The lesson could begin.

Mr Andrews gave out his instructions. They were to read the section beginning on page 96 about immigration, and then they were to make notes on it.

Delroy opened his book at the right page and began to read. It was something about black people coming to Britain from the West Indies in the 1950s and 1960s to work on the buses and in hospitals. There were pictures of smil-

3

ing West Indians wearing huge ties and absurdly long jackets. Delroy read the words underneath the photographs. Gradually, he found himself slowing down. He wasn't taking the words in. His mind was beginning to wander from the page.

It was too quiet in the classroom. He couldn't work when it was so quiet. It made him feel restless and uneasy. He noticed that his nails were getting long. He took out his nail-clippers and began to trim them. He was careful to keep his hands below the level of his desk so that Mr Andrews wouldn't see what he was doing.

A question formed itself in his mind. It buzzed there like a persistent fly that he couldn't flick away. It often came to him at moments like this when he was bored with work. Why did they refer to him as black? He looked at his own hands. The skin was brown. It was the colour of the mahogany he was using to make a table with in woodwork. He turned his hand over. The palm was even lighter. It was almost pink. He wouldn't describe himself as black at all. Yet that's what he was called. It had always seemed strange to him.

He examined the other boys in the class. Half of them were black. Some of them were darker than he was — as dark as plain chocolate or coffee without milk, Delroy thought. Others were paler — more the colour of honey or golden sand or leather. They all had the same kind of hair — crinkly black hair clinging closely to the scalp. Except for one boy whose hair was ginger.

The other boys in the class were Asian or white. The Asians had straight black hair and pale brown faces. The white boys were pink and pale and pasty-looking. Delroy didn't have much to do with them. All his friends were black, like himself. He had never been inside the house of an Asian or white boy — not even when he had been at junior school.

What did it matter anyway? He didn't care what other people said. He preferred the colour he was. After all, black was beautiful, wasn't it? But he still couldn't quite understand why he was called black when really he was brown.

4

Most of the other boys in the class were working. Stephen, the biggest black boy there, had already started making notes. That was just like Stephen. He always worked. He never messed about. If the others played around, Stephen sometimes got annoyed with them and told them to stop it. And because Stephen was so big, they usually did.

Stephen was very dark-skinned, like shining coal. He could certainly be called black. Delroy remembered a joke one of his friends had made about Stephen. He had said, 'There's black and black and Stephen Henry.' But he hadn't dared make the gibe in front of Stephen's face. No one would. Yes, Stephen was black all right.

Delroy had finished clipping his nails. He tried to get back to his book, but he couldn't concentrate on it. Why were they always on about immigration anyway? They were always making laws and regulations about it. Once someone had asked Mr Andrews how many black immigrants there were in Britain, and the teacher had said about three per cent. Delroy had been amazed that the number was so small. 'What are they so scared for then?' he had asked. Because everyone did seem to be scared. Everyone seemed to be terrified that there were going to be riots and violence all over the place if they let any more immigrants in. Every time anything happened it was blared out on television and there were huge headlines on the front pages of the newspapers. It didn't make sense.

People sometimes called him an immigrant, but he had been born here. He was as British as the next man. Jamaica was only a name to him. He had never been there. He had only his parents' stories to build up a picture of that island with its blue skies, sand and sugar cane, of throwing sticks to knock the mangoes off their branches, and waiting for the pears to drop ripe from the trees.

His parents were immigrants, he supposed. They had come to Britain in the 1960s. But they didn't work on the buses or in a hospital. His father was a salesman with a good job, and his mother was a junior school teacher. Why did people always have to think that immigrants were poor or spent their time scrounging off social security?

5

Delroy's thoughts were interrupted by a knock at the door. The door opened and a boy entered. All heads were raised as one from their work and swivelled round, eyes fixed on the boy. They followed his progress as he made his way between the rows of desks to Mr Andrews.

'Please, sir,' the boy said, 'the headmaster wants to see Delroy Ellis immediately.'

There were some cheers and guffaws at this as the pupils all turned to look at Delroy.

'Stop that,' shouted Mr Andrews threateningly. 'Don't you know how to behave properly? If someone comes into the classroom, he comes to talk to me, not to you.'

He surveyed the black, brown and white faces in front of him. The pupils returned his gaze sullenly, then dropped their eyes and continued with their work — all except Delroy.

'Right, Ellis,' said Mr Andrews, 'you'd better go and see the head straightaway. What have you been up to this time, I wonder?'

Delroy didn't answer. He wasn't sure what the answer was. There were so many things he had done wrong that the headmaster might want to talk to him about.

He rose from his seat and followed the boy out of the room. On his way down to the headmaster's office he went through all the possible reasons for this summons. There had been that fight in the playground yesterday. Could it be that? He had been late for school three times last week. He had gone out of school during lunch break the previous day to buy some biscuits from the corner shop. That was against the school rules. Had someone seen him? Perhaps it was just going to be a general moan about his poor work and lack of progress.

Delroy was frowning deeply, partly with the effort of trying to work out which of his many sins had been discovered, and partly because he felt nervous at having to see the headmaster. It was worrying enough to be sent for by the head — it was even worse not knowing what it was about.

He hesitated outside the door of the head's office, putting off the moment when he had to knock. It was as bad as going to the dentist. At last he took a deep breath and rapped on the door with his knuckles. The sound was firm, much more confident than he felt. A voice from inside shouted, 'Come in!'

When Delroy saw that Mr Frobisher was with the head, his memory came flooding back. Now he knew why he had been sent for. He hadn't considered yesterday's piece of bother with Mr Frobisher. It was the sort of thing that might have been reported to his form teacher. He hadn't expected Mr Frobisher to go to the head about it. That was a mean thing to do.

Mr Johnson, the headmaster, was sitting behind his desk. When he saw Delroy, he leaned back in his chair, and his body slumped wearily.

'Oh dear,' he sighed. 'Here we are again, Delroy, eh?'

'What, sir?' asked Delroy, keeping very still, his head bowed and his eyes darting quick looks to take in the expressions on the faces of Mr Frobisher and the headmaster.

Mr Frobisher was tall and thin. He held himself rigidly, like a soldier at attention, except that his arms were folded with neat precision across his chest. His eyes were concentrating hard on Delroy. Mr Johnson by contrast was small and round and rather untidy looking. He gave the impression of being tired, and his hair always looked as though he had forgotten to comb it. He was not the kind of figure Delroy expected a headmaster to be. But he smiled a lot, and Delroy was grateful for that.

'I think you know what this is about,' continued Mr Johnson.

'No, sir,' said Delroy innocently.

'Well, I've had a complaint from Mr Frobisher about your behaviour at the end of school yesterday. It appears that Mr Frobisher asked you to pick up some paper from the floor and you refused.'

Mr Frobisher burst in angrily. 'He behaved disgracefully. He just wouldn't do it. When I asked him again he started being abusive. Finally, he stormed out of the oom, knocking two chairs over. I called him back, but he just ignored me. I can't accept that kind of behaviour. I'm not

7

going to stand being defied in that way.'

There was nothing new in Mr Frobisher's complaints. Delroy could list a whole series of incidents when he had been caught out by Mr Frobisher — or provoked by him. That was it. Mr Frobisher provoked you into behaving badly. You might be doing nothing at all, just minding your own business, and Mr Frobisher would come along and accuse you of doing something wrong, and you got indignant and lost your temper, and he had you. He was always trying to get you.

Delroy's face grew hard and his eyes flared up.

'It's not my job to pick up paper off the floor,' he said as angrily as Mr Frobisher. 'I'm not his slave. Anyway, why me? He's always picking on me. Cha!'

Delroy rolled his head away from Mr Frobisher and sucked his teeth in utter contempt.

'There,' said Mr Frobisher, turning to the headmaster. 'You see how he talks to me. The boy's in endless trouble. He never does what he's told. He gets away with murder. It's time he was put in his place and taught who's boss in this school.'

Delroy's whole body was stiff now, his fists clenching and unclenching at his sides. He felt that if he became any more tense his bones would snap in two.

'Why should I pick up his paper?' he demanded. 'He only asked me because I'm black. He wouldn't ask a white boy to do it. He's always picking on the black boys in the class.'

'Oh, God,' sneered Mr Frobisher, 'we're getting that old chestnut, are we?' Then he turned threatening. 'Don't you try that one on me. I've heard them all.'

Delroy felt himself being wound up. It was always the same with Mr Frobisher. He would attack and attack until the pupil retaliated. And then, of course, the pupil was in trouble for giving as good as he got. The teacher could do it, but the pupil couldn't. Delroy knew this, and yet he couldn't hold himself back. He was about to return Mr Frobisher's threats when Mr Johnson prevented him.

'Leave it with me, Mr Frobisher,' the headmaster said, at the same time conciliatory and resigned. 'I'll try to make Delroy see sense and sort something out.'

Mr Frobisher looked dissatisfied with this proposal. He hesitated and seemed about to give vent to some more angry words. Then he turned and left the office without saying anything.

Delroy waited to see what would happen next. Mr Johnson rose and came round to the front of his desk. He stood leaning against the edge, his arms folded, his eyes fixed steadily on Delroy.

'You do get into some trouble, don't you, Delroy?' he said quietly. His tone was a mixture of concern, sympathy and amusement.

Delroy's eyes flickered upwards to take a quick look at the headmaster. Mr Johnson appeared completely at ease. He wasn't angry. He didn't seem to be taking the incident very seriously. Certainly he wasn't threatening in any way. Delroy allowed his body to relax. A half-ashamed smile played about his mouth.

'Come and sit down,' said Mr Johnson, pushing him gently in the direction of a chair, 'and we'll talk about it.'

Delroy was still feeling a little sulky, but now he had himself under control. With Mr Frobisher gone, his anger had evaporated. He was prepared to be more reasonable.

'Why wouldn't you pick up the paper when Mr Frobisher asked you to?' Mr Johnson inquired mildly. 'It seems a perfectly reasonable request to make.'

'It's not my job,' said Delroy. 'What do you have cleaners for?'

'Yes,' agreed Mr Johnson, 'but you should try to be helpful. I don't see why their job should be made more difficult than it has to be. We expect boys in this school to be co-operative and help to keep the place clean and pleasant. If I see a crisp packet or a sweet wrapper in the corridor, I pick it up and put it in the bin.'

'I didn't put the paper there,' said Delroy, trying another excuse.

'That's got nothing to do with it,' said Mr Johnson. 'We expect all boys to help. If I had asked you to do it, you wouldn't have refused, would you?'

Delroy thought for a while. 'You'd have asked me

politely. Mr Frobisher just yells at you. He thinks he's God or something.'

'In this world you have to learn to get on with all kinds of people. That's part of what growing up is all about.'

'Yes, but he doesn't have to yell at me.'

'He yells at me sometimes,' said Mr Johnson ruefully.

Delroy couldn't help smiling at the thought of the headmaster being shouted at by one of his own teachers. But he wasn't sure whether or not Mr Johnson was just making it up.

'That's better,' said the headmaster, and he smiled. 'Now then. What are we going to do about all this?'

Delroy's smile faded and he waited anxiously. He knew some kind of bitter pill was coming.

'First of all,' said Mr Johnson, 'I think Mr Frobisher deserves an apology.'

Delroy looked at the head dubiously but said nothing. Apologize to Mr Frobisher? As far as Delroy was concerned, Mr Frobisher ought to apologize to him.

'After all, he was only doing his job, helping to keep the place clean by asking you to pick the paper up. And he's not there for you to lose your temper with and be sworn at.'

'I didn't swear at him,' said Delroy quickly. Why did people always get the facts wrong?

'Well, whatever you did, you weren't being very pleasant. You've upset him.'

'He upset me,' said Delroy, pretending indignation.

'Calm down,' said Mr Johnson. 'I know it's difficult, but it's sometimes the best way. Often I have to apologize to people even when I think they are the ones in the wrong. It doesn't cost me anything, and it helps to keep the wheels oiled.'

Delroy was still uncertain. There was a struggle in his mind between standing up for himself or losing face.

'Can you manage it?' Mr Johnson asked.

'I suppose so,' said Delroy with poor grace. He wasn't sure that he could.

'You've got to do it properly — at least look as if you mean it.'

'Yes.'

'Come along then, let's see if we can find Mr Frobisher and get it over with.'

Mr Frobisher was teaching, and Mr Johnson called him to the door of the classroom.

'I've had a long talk with Delroy,' he told the teacher, 'and he wants to apologize for his behaviour yesterday.'

Mr Frobisher's face was hard and stony. Delroy frowned at him. He felt Mr Johnson's hand on his shoulder.

'What have you got to say, Delroy?' the headmaster coaxed.

Delroy lowered his head and mumbled, 'Sorry, sir.'

'That's all very well,' said Mr Frobisher, 'but I think he ought to be punished as well. How can I be expected to control my classes if he defies me in front of other boys and gets away with it?'

Delroy scowled at Mr Frobisher and was about to reply when he felt the pressure of Mr Johnson's hand on his shoulder increase.

'He can have a school detention as well then,' said Mr Johnson. 'Is that enough?' It seemed to Delroy that the headmaster's voice was rather cool.

'I think that's the least that should happen,' said Mr Frobisher.

'All right, Delroy,' said Mr Johnson. 'School detention.'

Delroy looked at the headmaster. His hand was still there.

'I suppose so,' he said.

But Mr Frobisher hadn't finished yet.

'I think a letter should go to his parents as well,' he said. 'I think they ought to know about the disgraceful way he behaves in school.'

At the mention of a letter, Delroy felt a cold clutch of fear in his stomach. Here it was. He had known it all along. What he had dreaded was going to happen again. He could imagine only too clearly how his father would react when he received yet another complaining letter from the school.

'Very well,' said Mr Johnson, 'if that's what you want.'

11

Delroy was allowed no say in the matter.

'Right,' said Mr Johnson to Delroy, 'you'd better get back to your class now. We don't want you to lose any more of your education.'

The headmaster released his hold.

There was nothing Delroy could do. The school was going to send the letter and that was the end of it. His parents would find out about his bad behaviour. His father would be angry. There was no telling what he might do this time. And it was all Mr Frobisher's fault.

TWO

Delroy was still brooding over the letter and his sense of injustice when his friends crowded round him at break, anxious to find out what had happened.

'How did it go?' asked Paul, his quarrel over the seat forgotten.

'What was it about?' asked Ant'ny.

''Ave you been suspended?' asked Bradman.

'No,' said Delroy. 'I had to apologize to Mr Frobisher, and I've got a school detention.'

'Oh, no!' exploded Ant'ny, his black face scowling with hostility towards authority. He was big and broad. Whenever boys were in trouble they came to him for advice. He believed in standing up for his rights, and the rights of other boys like him. 'Oh, no!' he repeated. 'That's not fair. Why should you 'ave to apologize to that pig? I wouldn't 'ave apologized.'

'And they're going to send a letter home,' Delroy went on, bringing up his major grievance. He turned hot and cold as he thought about it — hot with anger at the school for sending the letter, and cold at the imagined scene at home when his father received it.

'I think you was lucky,' said Bradman. He was smaller than Ant'ny, with a cheeky face. He knew how to use his charm to keep out of trouble. 'Boys 'ave been suspended for less than that.'

12

'Yeah,' said Ant'ny, 'too many boys get suspended too often at this school for not'in' at all. It's dread, man.'

'Sending a letter home's just as bad as suspension,' muttered Delroy miserably.

'No, I think you was let off lightly,' said Bradman.

'Yeah, Mr Johnson's soft,' jeered Paul.

''E's always soft,' said Ant'ny with contempt.

'Thank you black skin 'e is,' said Bradman.

'Who you callin' black, guy?' demanded Ant'ny, putting on his Jamaican voice. 'Get back in the oven.'

Bradman took up the familiar game of insults. 'Aw, shut you mout', crepe-hair,' he snarled.

'Is you talkin' to I?' demanded Ant'ny with mock disbelief. 'Is you talkin' to I?'

'I don' see no one else 'round I's talkin' to' said Bradman with a pretence of dignified indifference.

Delroy's gloomy mood began to lift. His face softened into a cheery grin as he joined in the play.

'It ain't nobody else 'round 'e talkin' to,' he said. ''E talkin' to you, liver lips.'

'Don' you call me that, man,' said Ant'ny, his eyes widening in a threat.

'Why not?' asked Delroy.

''Cos I'll mash you up if you do,' warned Ant'ny.

Delroy and Bradman threw themselves about with laughter.

'You an' who else?' spluttered Bradman.

'Me an' nobody else,' said Ant'ny, putting on a show of anger and stretching his arms out in a gesture like Frankenstein's monster about to seize a victim.

'You couldn' mash nobody,' said Bradman scornfully.

'Yeah, you couldn' mash nobody,' repeated Delroy.

Ant'ny was lost for words. No reply would come. He stood there, rigid, breathing out indignation, still as part of the game.

'You refugee,' said Bradman, adding a further insult.

'You foreigner,' said Paul.

'Yeah,' jeered Delroy. 'Yeah.' He searched around for another insult he could pile on top of Ant'ny. He found it. 'Yeah,' he said, 'you immigrant.'

13

'Yeah,' yelled Bradman, 'get back on the banana boat.'

At last, Ant'ny reacted. He leaped in the air and aimed a Kung Fu chop at his friend. Delroy grinned widely and backed away.

'You immigrant,' he cried again and he doubled himself up with laugher.

Then he was off across the playground with Ant'ny in hot pursuit. The two boys barged their way through the horde of frenzied footballers. Delroy kept grinning, looking over his shoulder to make sure that Ant'ny was out of striking distance. Ant'ny kept making lunges, his arms outstretched, to try to catch him.

Finally, Delroy turned. The two boys soared upwards, their arms and legs shooting out and twisting round, missing each other by inches. Honour satisfied, they stood there, panting and grinning at each other.

Some small boys playing football passed them. Delroy had recovered his breath. He chased after them. One boy was pushed out of his path, and the other was blocked. With the ball at his feet, Delroy dribbled the full length of the playground, elbowing other players out of the way, feinting and turning back on himself before he shot the ball against the wall.

'Goal!' he yelled.

He cheered wildly and ran round the playground, throwing himself into the air every few steps and punching his fist at the sky. He had completely forgotten about his trouble with Mr Frobisher — and about the letter.

THREE

At the end of school, Delroy waited at the gate for his friends. They always waited for each other and went down to the shopping centre together. That was where they usually caught the bus home. At least that was the excuse. They didn't catch the first bus that came — or the second, or the third. There was too much going on in the shopping

14

centre to make them want to go straight home. Or at any rate there was the chance that something would happen. Standing around was in itself a kind of excitement. You never knew what would turn up to make the day worthwhile. Anyway, there was nothing to hurry home for.

Ant'ny arrived, pushing a path through a throng of smaller boys hurrying out of school.

'You been in trouble 'gain this afternoon?' he asked Delroy.

'Naw,' replied Delroy. 'I'm bein' a good boy.'

'Who's been suspended then?' asked Bradman eagerly as he drew up to them.

'Nobody I've heard of,' said Delroy.

'Somet'in's wrong,' pronounced Ant'ny darkly. 'Either they're gettin' soft or we losin' our touch.'

Paul raced down on them and went on past.

'Come on, guys,' he cried, and they chased after him.

Delroy heard his name called. It was Stephen.

'Don't forget the practice tomorrow night,' Stephen said.

'O.K.' said Delroy.

Stephen went on his way in the opposite direction. He was captain of the basketball team. He never went down to the shopping centre after school. He always went straight home.

'What you playin' basketball for?' demanded Ant'ny as they moved on.

'I like it,' said Delroy.

'I wouldn' play for the school team, not if they paid me,' said Bradman.

'They wouldn' 'ave you,' teased Paul.

'Oh yeah they would,' retorted Bradman. 'I used to be in the team.'

'You used to *be* the team,' said Ant'ny mockingly.

'That's right,' said Bradman, smiling. 'They're no good now I left.'

'Now you thrown out,' corrected Paul.

'They're no good now I gone,' said Bradman complacently. 'There ain't a rankin' player 'mong 'em.'

'Stephen's good,' defended Delroy.

'Aw, Stephen,' sneered Ant'ny. ''E too goody-goody for anyt'in'. What you wants to mix wit' 'im for?'

'Anyway' said Bradman, 'I wouldn' play for the school.'

'Yeah,' said Ant'ny to Delroy. 'Why don' you drop out? You want they pat you on the 'ead or somet'in'?'

'They don' do not'in' fo' you, so why you do somet'in' fo' them?' asked Bradman.

'I like it,' repeated Delroy.

Delroy had had this conversation before. His friends were always trying to get him to stop playing for the school. And he could see that in a way he was letting them down by staying in the team. It was not through any sense of loyalty to the school. He simply enjoyed playing — the excitement, the speed, the physical exhaustion, the delight of winning. He was also good at it. That made a difference. He enjoyed showing off his skill. And, although he didn't like admitting it, there were times when he liked getting a bit of praise. It made a change from complaints and detentions.

By now they had reached the shopping centre. They made for a bench which was their usual base. Two small boys sitting there scurried away as Delroy and his friends approached. They took over.

'Who's got some fags?' Bradman demanded.

'I 'aven't got none,' said Ant'ny. 'I don' smoke.'

'I'm dying for a drag,' said Bradman. ''Ow much money we got?'

The boys turned out their pockets to pool their resources. The total didn't come to enough for a packet of cigarettes. Bradman looked around the people walking up and down the shopping centre.

'Just a minute,' he said, and jumped up.

He stopped a younger boy who was passing at that moment.

'Look,' he said. ''Ave you got any money?'

The small boy immediately looked frightened and began to back away.

'Come 'ere,' said Bradman, taking hold of the boy by the lapel of his blazer. 'I need ten pence. 'Ave you got it?

I'll let you 'ave it back.'

At those words Bradman's friends, who were watching, burst out laughing. The boy became even more frightened.

'I've only got the money for my bus fare,' he stammered.

''Ow much is that?' Bradman asked.

'Ten pence,' said the boy.

'That'll do,' said Bradman. ''And it over.'

The small boy fumbled in his pocket.

''Urry up,' said Bradman impatiently. He began to shake the boy backwards and forwards.

At last the boy found his ten pence piece and held it out.

Bradman took the coin. 'Thanks,' he said casually. 'I'll give it back to you some time. Make sure you ask me for it.'

Delroy and the others hooted again. They danced up and down and clicked their fingers in the air.

'Yeah,' said Delroy. 'You make sure you ask him for it.'

'Come on,' said Bradman. 'Let's get some fags.'

They followed Bradman towards the newsagent's. The small boy was left looking lost and tearful on the pavement.

With Bradman in the lead, the boys went into the shop. As soon as the man behind the counter saw them, a look of panic swept across his face.

'There are too many of you,' he shouted. 'I can't have you all in the shop at the same time.'

'What d'you mean?' demanded Ant'ny. 'We've as much right to be 'ere as anyone else. We want to buy somet'in'. Our money's as good as other people's, innit?'

'Yeah,' said Delroy, rising to the shopkeeper's hostility. 'What's wrong with our money?'

'What d'you want then?' the man asked, anxious to be rid of them.

The boys studiously began to examine the goods on display. They spread out through the shop. The man had difficulty keeping them all in view at the same time.

'Hurry up,' he said. 'I haven't got all day.'

'I can' see no other customers,' said Ant'ny haughtily.

'Never mind other customers,' said the shopkeeper. 'What do you want?'

Bradman named his brand of cigarettes.

To get the cigarettes, the shopkeeper had to reach for a shelf behind him. He tried to do it without turning his back on the boys. He wasn't entirely successful. There was one split second when he had to use his eyes to locate the cigarettes and direct his fingers to pick them up. In that split second Bradman's hand shot out, and a bar of chocolate disappeared from the stack on the counter into his pocket. His eyes didn't so much as blink. Delroy gazed at him with admiration.

The shopkeeper was careful to take the money before handing the cigarettes over. He continued to watch the boys suspiciously, his eyes darting from one to another, trying to keep them all under surveillance. He held the money in his hand. He wasn't going to risk putting it in the till before the boys had gone.

Bradman and the others lingered. They picked up magazines and leafed through them. They examined the crisps and sweets in a display stand, making it revolve. They looked in the ice-cream cabinet. All the while the shopkeeper watched them nervously. The boys knew he was watching. They knew he was nervous. They enjoyed taking their time. It was all part of the game.

'You've got what you came for,' said the shopkeeper at last. 'Now you'd better go.'

'All right,' said Ant'ny. 'If you don' want our money.'

'We'll go and spend it somewhere else then,' said Delroy.

'I don' know 'ow you make a profit, man,' said Bradman. 'Still, if you want to turn good customers away. . . .'

Very slowly, as though they had all the time in the world, the boys left the shop. Ant'ny was last. As he turned to go out he gave the shopkeeper a long, menacing stare that would have fused the lights on a Christmas tree. It was one of his specialities. Many a teacher had quailed before it.

Outside, they immediately lit up.

'I've been waitin' for that all day,' said Bradman. 'I'd just started one this morning at break when old Watson came in, and I 'ad to throw it down the bog. What a waste!'

He puffed away at the cigarette as though his life depended on it.

Ant'ny stamped up and down impatiently. He had no time for cigarettes. 'What 'bout that chocolate then?' he demanded.

''Ere you are,' said Bradman, taking the bar out of his pocket and handing it to Ant'ny. 'Don' eat it all.'

Ant'ny examined it with disgust. 'You know I don' like chocolate wit' nuts in,' he said. He nevertheless hurriedly crammed a couple of squares of the chocolate into his mouth.

'There's no pleasin' some people,' said Bradman resignedly.

While they had been inside the shop, a panda car had drawn up opposite the bus-stop. Inside were two policemen gazing expressionlessly in front of them.

'Watch out,' warned Bradman. 'The pigs are 'ere.'

The boys turned their equally impassive faces to stare at the policemen as they walked past the car. This was part of another game they played — though game was not exactly the right word to describe it. They took with deadly seriousness this show of coolness which merely emphasised their hostility. A state of war existed. The police were the enemy. All the boys could give examples of how they or their friends had been victims of police harassment. Whenever the police arrived on the scene, defences were put up, and sharp-eyed watchfulness was on parade. The name of the game was to sail as close to dumb insolence as they dared.

At the top of the street they stopped, turned and began to retrace their steps, faces and eyes directed with cold intensity towards the panda car.

But before they had reached the car, their interest was diverted. Further up the road some kind of disturbance had broken out. There were shouts; a crowd was beginning to collect.

19

'It's a fight!' cried Ant'ny, and the boys hurried eagerly to join the excitement. They were followed by the two policemen who had snapped to attention abruptly and jumped out of their car.

Shoving through a mass of giggling and shrieking girls, Delroy felt his spirits rise as he saw two young men squaring up aggressively to each other. They were both black and both sharply dressed. Their faces glowered at each other. A girl tried to pull one of them away, but he shrugged her off without even looking at her. He pushed his opponent in the chest so that he staggered back. Regaining his balance, the other man raised his arm ready to charge into the attack. And then the policemen arrived to spoil it.

'What's going on here?' one of them demanded.

Immediately the scene was transformed. The two fighters dropped their hostile stances and relaxed. Their faces lit up with smiles.

'Not'in', not'in',' said one of them, putting his arm round his opponent's shoulders as though they were the best of friends. 'Soft, man, soft. We was just 'avin' a argument.'

'That right,' said the other. 'Just a friendly argument.'

'Then have it somewhere else,' said the policeman. 'Move on.'

'Sure, sure. We just goin'. Right?'

Still smiling and laughing, the two men walked off around the corner. A crowd of chattering girls followed them. The policemen were left looking suspiciously after them, feeling cheated.

The excitement over, Delroy and his friends went back to their bench. They felt good. Something had happened to break the monotony of the afternoon. They began to discuss the fight and joke about it. Then they sensed the shadows of the two policemen weighing upon them.

'What are you boys hanging around here for?' one of the policemen asked.

The boys carefully kept their eyes away from the policemen and pretended they hadn't heard. The police-

20

man who had spoken moved round in front of them and repeated his question. Ant'ny looked at him remotely as though pondering some deep philosophical problem. Was he really there? Was he really a human being like other people?

'We're waitin' for a bus,' he said at last.

'Which one?'

'The 52.'

'There have been two 52s through here in the last ten minutes.'

'We're choosy which bus we get,' said Ant'ny, daring the policemen to do something about it.

The policeman spoke grimly. 'You'd better get on the next 52 that comes along or else there will be trouble.'

'We can sit here if we like, can't we?' said Delroy. 'We're not doing anybody any harm. It's a free country, isn't it?'

The two policemen directed their full attention on Delroy.

'What did you say?' one of them asked.

'Cool it, man,' said Bradman urgently to Delroy.

But Delroy wasn't to be advised. 'We can wait here if we like,' he said. 'We don't have to get the next bus if we don't want to.'

'Get in that car,' said the first policeman, his eyes narrowed and his mouth tense.

Delroy stayed where he was. His feet were fixed to the ground. He wasn't sure that he could have moved even if he had wanted to. He had a strange sensation of weightlessness. It was as though his body didn't exist. There was just his mind, wavering between fear and defiance.

'Did you hear what I said?' asked the policeman, his voice low with menace.

Delroy still didn't move. He couldn't think what his reply should be. But he was saved from making a decision. The policeman suddenly seized him by the lapels of his jacket and jerked him up from the bench.

'Do what you are told,' he ordered.

Delroy was propelled from behind towards the panda car. The door was opened. The front seat was pulled for-

21

ward and he was thrust into the back. The policeman who had manhandled him got into the front seat. The other stood outside, facing Delroy's friends who had also moved towards the car and were glowering at the policemen.

Delroy's face shut tight. It was shut like a wall — to protect him from whatever the policeman was going to do or say, and to prevent the resentment and anger burning within him from bursting out.

The policeman leaned over the back of his seat and put his face very close to Delroy's.

'You had better get one thing straight,' he said slowly and threateningly. 'If a policeman tells you to do something, you do it. You don't argue the toss. Understand?'

Delroy stared angrily at the fat, white face towering over his own. So furious was his hate that he felt as though steam were pouring out of his nostrils.

'Don't try and play clever tricks with me, nigger boy,' the policeman went on, 'because you won't succeed.'

Delroy's eyes flinched at the insult, and his body stiffened. The policeman noticed the change in his attitude and grew wary.

'Have you been in trouble with the police before?' he asked.

Delroy managed to shake his head.

'I think I'd better make sure,' said the policeman. He took out his notebook. 'What's your name and address?'

Delroy replied as briefly as possible while the policeman wrote the facts down.

'I'll check this up at the station,' he said. 'And remember,' he added, his face coming close again, 'your name and address have been noted. If there's any more trouble from you, you're for the chop.'

The policeman got out and shoved the front seat up.

'Now, get out of here before you make me sick.'

Delroy stumbled into the fresh air, glad to gasp great gulpfuls of it after the vile atmosphere of the car. He joined his friends on the pavement, and they stood watching, disapprovingly, as the policemen got in the car and drove off.

'Bastards,' muttered Bradman.

'Pigs!' shouted Ant'ny, and he threw his fist in the air in a gesture of defiance after them.

'What did he say?' asked Paul.

'They just took my name and address,' said Delroy.

'Did they touch you?' asked Ant'ny. 'Lay a finger on you?'

'No,' said Delroy, 'nothing like that.'

He didn't feel like talking about it. He wasn't sure that he could trust himself. If he opened his mouth to say what he really felt, all that would come out would be a torrent of incoherent and angry abuse.

Then there was another thought that preoccupied him. It gnawed away at his mind like a grub burrowing into the flesh of a rotting apple. Suppose the police got in touch with his parents. Suppose they stirred things up and told lies about him. They were capable of anything. There was still the letter from school about his misbehaviour to be faced. That was bad enough. To have the police knocking at the door would be even worse. He could imagine only too well how his father would react. He would be most anxious and helpful in front of the police, but as soon as they were gone, and father and son were left together. . . .

The next 52 bus was drawing into the precinct. The boys suddenly came to life again.

'There's the bus,' yelled Ant'ny.

They jumped up and raced into the road. Before the bus had come to a halt at the bus-stop, Ant'ny and Brad-man were clinging to the hand-bar, their legs swinging wildly in the air.

There was a crowd of shoppers at the bus-stop, laden with heavy bags and baskets. They let off angry shouts of protest and complaints.

'Get in the queue, you!'

'Stop pushing in!'

But by then, Ant'ny and Bradman were already scrambling up the stairs.

The Asian bus conductor arrived at the entrance and tried to restore some kind of order. Delroy and Paul lowered their heads and shoved their way through the crowd. One woman's bag fell to the ground. A cabbage and several potatoes rolled out. Stooping to retrieve her goods, the woman was almost trampled under foot. The conductor shouted for people to stop pushing and tried to prevent the crowd from boarding the bus until the chaos had been sorted out.

Paul and Delroy ignored him. They shouldered their way past and shot up the stairs.

'Bloody Paki,' muttered Delroy. 'Who does he think he is?'

Settled into their seats, they lit up cigarettes and began to relax. They reminisced about the events of the afternoon.

'Bloody fuzz,' said Ant'ny, 'throwin' their weight around.'

Bradman pulled on his cigarette. He inhaled the smoke and released it in a powerful, narrow stream. He considered it as it merged with the atmosphere.

'You know,' he said. 'They didn' get what they come for.'

'How d'you mean?' asked Ant'ny.

'You should 'ave seen their faces when those two guys stop fightin'. It really put their noses out o' joint.'

Slowly, Ant'ny started to laugh. Soon the others were joining in. There was no stopping them. No matter how they tried they went on laughing until their sides ached. Delroy could feel tears running down his cheeks and wiped them away with his hand. Passengers in front turned round to see what the disturbance was, but that only made the boys laugh even louder.

FOUR

Delroy lay in bed. His eyes were screwed tight against the light coming through the curtains. When he moved his head, he could feel the icy chill of the pillow against his cheek. His nose, sticking out above the bedclothes, was numb. He curled himself up into a ball so as to keep himself as warm as possible. At any moment he knew that he would hear his mother's voice calling up the stairs, telling him it was time to get up. Already there were noises below as water was run, juddering the pipes, and cups were rattled in their saucers. He allowed himself to sink into that luxurious state that wasn't quite sleep and wasn't quite consciousness, before getting up to start the day.

Dreams flickered behind his hard-shut eyes. He wasn't certain if they were real or merely fantasies. Had he been awakened during the night? Had he heard voices raised in the room below? He had a feeling that his father had come home late, that there had been a row. His mother had been angry. The loud voices and fierce accusations had carried through the house. He had heard his own name mentioned, his father calling it out in angry debate. 'That boy is always in trouble. I've had enough of him. That's an end of it. I don't want to have anything more to do with him.' There had been tears too — the sound of his mother crying and sobbing. And then silence.

Had it been real or only a dream? Delroy wasn't sure. He tried to shake off the visions and sink once more into the warmth of sleep. But then a voice calling from below brought him to the surface again.

'Delroy, it's time you were up. You're going to be late.'

It was his mother. It was the first time she had summoned him. There was no need yet to desert his comforting coma.

Suddenly, the incident with Mr Frobisher swam into his mind, and Delroy was wide awake. There was that letter they were going to send. It would tell his parents all about it. There would be more rows.

Five days had passed since the incident, and the letter had not yet arrived. Each morning, Delroy had looked out urgently to see if it had come. Surely it must be delivered today if it was to arrive at all.

He threw the bedclothes back and stood up. He did not notice now the coldness of the air around him. In bare feet he tiptoed to the door and opened it. He crept to the top of the stairs from which he could see the front door. The mat was bare. Either the postman had not yet arrived, or it was already too late.

25

Delroy hurried to the bathroom. He wiped his face with a damp flannel and passed the toothbrush over his teeth. On his way back to his bedroom, he had another look to see if any letters were lying on the mat. It was still bare.

He took off his pyjamas and pulled on his school clothes, making as much speed as possible. He was just going down the stairs to the kitchen when a shadow darkened the glass of the front door and some letters were dropped through the letter-box. For a moment Delroy froze, wondering if anyone else had heard the gentle thud of the letters on the mat. There seemed to be no change in the sounds of activity coming from the kitchen. Without stopping to think, Delroy ran down the remaining stairs to the front door. He picked the letters up. There were three of them. One was a hand-written envelope addressed to his parents. The second was an official form of some kind. The third was a buff-coloured envelope with his parents' name and address typed on it. It had a local post-mark. Delroy was certain it was the letter from school.

He looked round to make sure that no one was watching. Then he put the buff envelope into the inside pocket of his blazer.

As he heard the kitchen door open he jumped nervously.

'There you are,' said his mother, seeming surprised. 'What's got you up so early this morning? I usually have to call you three times before you bother to come down.'

'I said I'd meet some friends before school,' explained Delroy, thinking quickly. 'The postman's been.'

He handed the remaining two letters to his mother.

'I'm glad your friends have got you up in time for once,' said Mrs Ellis. 'But don't let them make you late for school.'

Delroy sat down to his breakfast. He noted that his mother was unusually quiet that morning. Normally she talked non-stop— about the weather, about what she was going to do during the day, about school, about the week-end, about relations, about things in the news. The rest of the family never answered, but that didn't seem to worry

26

her. Today, she put bacon silently into the frying-pan and broke eggs into a basin. The only sound that could be heard was from the sizzling pan. Delroy began to think that the row he had heard in the night had not been his imagination.

He was halfway through his cornflakes when his father appeared.

Mr Ellis was slim and well-dressed. He could easily have been thought ten years younger than his real age. He took a great pride in his appearance.

Father and son looked at each other but said nothing. Mrs Ellis pushed the two letters in front of her husband, and he opened them and began to read.

Then she went to the kitchen door and called out, 'Barry, you're going to be late.'

There was a muffled answer from upstairs.

Delroy had nearly finished his bacon and eggs when Barry, his younger brother, arrived.

'Good morning, Barry,' beamed Mr Ellis. 'How's my boy then?'

'All right, Dad,' said Barry. He slumped into his chair and began to attack the cornflakes already poured for him.

'When's your next football match?' Mr Ellis asked.

'Tomorrow night, after school,' said Barry.

'Are you going to beat them?'

'Yes, of course.'

'You'd better score some goals.'

'I will. I'm going to get two at least.'

Mr Ellis laughed indulgently.

'You'd better hurry up, Barry,' said his mother, 'or you're going to be late.'

'I can give you a lift into school today,' said Mr Ellis. 'I'm going that way.'

He turned to Delroy. 'Do you want a lift?' Delroy was aware that his father's tone was noticeably cooler.

'No thanks,' said Delroy flatly. 'I'm meeting someone.'

'So long as it's not that Bradman,' said Mr Ellis. 'I've told you not to mix with him.'

Delroy didn't reply. He got up from the table.

27

'And make sure you're home early tonight,' went on Mr Ellis. 'Straight home from school. I'm not having you come in at all hours.'

Delroy still didn't say anything. He went into the hall to collect his bag. His mother followed him. She put her arm round him.

'All right, Delroy?' she asked.

'Yes,' he replied.

'We'll see you tonight then,' she said, and he left the house.

He turned out of the gate and into the road. As soon as he thought the coast was clear, he took the letter from his pocket. He tore it open and read it as he walked slowly forward.

'Dear Mr and Mrs Ellis,' it said. 'I regret to inform you that your son Delroy was involved in an unpleasant incident yesterday. He disobeyed a teacher and was deliberately rude to him. He has now apologized and has been given a school detention because of his rudeness. I am sure that you will agree with me that pupils should treat teachers with respect. I hope you will enforce upon Delroy the need for politeness at all times. Please 'phone the school to make an appointment to come and see me so that we can discuss Delroy's behaviour and progress.' The letter was signed by the headmaster.

After reading the letter, Delroy stared at it blindly. His mind seethed with anger. The headmaster had said that he was going to send a letter telling his parents what he had done, but he hadn't said he was going to ask his parents to go up to the school to discuss it. By seizing the letter, Delroy thought that he could destroy the evidence, that his parents need never know about the row with Mr Frobisher, and it could be forgotten. Now there was a complication. If his parents didn't contact the school as the letter said, then the school might get on to his parents. He just couldn't win.

'The bastard,' Delroy said out loud, giving vent to his feelings. 'They're all bastards.'

He screwed the letter up into a ball in his hands. He didn't care. They could do what they liked.

There was a grating in the roadway at the edge of the pavement. Delroy put his bag down and forced the scrunched up paper between the bars. He stood for a moment looking at the grating through which the letter had disappeared, his mouth compressed in fury. Then he picked his bag up and hurried off to meet Bradman.

FIVE

Bradman's house was quite different from Delroy's. He lived in a council flat. It was on the fifth floor of a large block, one of several set in a concrete landscape. The lifts were always out of order. To get to the flat, Delroy had to climb flight after flight of stairs. At night it was spooky. The lights were always broken. At this hour of the morning it was still half-dark, and Delroy had to sidle along the wall, edging upwards step by step. He had to wade through the litter which was everywhere — plastic bags, newspapers, cigarette packets, food cartons. There was a dank, sour smell. It was as though every cat and dog in the area came to do their business there. Perhaps people as well, Delroy thought with a shudder of distaste. He was relieved when he emerged into the fresh air on the landings. As he approached them, he could see that the stair wells were covered with spray paint and graffiti.

'Spurs Forever'
'N F = Nazi Filth'
'Linda 4 Mike'
were some of the statements emblazoned on the walls.

Delroy pressed the bell to Bradman's flat. From here he could see across to the other concrete monsters, and beyond them street upon street of houses sliding down the slope of the hill. He pressed the bell again.

Eventually the door was opened by a woman wearing a head-square and holding a small baby. It was the wife or girl-friend — Delroy wasn't sure which — of one of Bradman's brothers. She looked as though she was still half-asleep.

'Bradman not up yet,' she said.

29

She moved back so that Delroy could enter.

'You know where 'e is?' she asked.

'Yes,' said Delroy, and he went along the passageway to Bradman's room.

There were two beds in the room, both of them occupied. In the large bed pushed into the corner, Delroy could make out the bulky shape of Bradman's brother, Errol, his broad black shoulders and arms bulging out of the bedclothes, his head punched into the pillow. When Delroy went in, Errol cranked his head up, squinted an eye open, grunted, and buried his head more deeply into the pillow again.

On the other bed, a narrow camp-bed just inside the door, lay Bradman, his mouth wide open, fast asleep.

The woman followed Delroy into the room. She took a tea-pot from the stove and poured herself a cup of tea. Still holding the baby, she sat down at the kitchen table.

'Bradman,' she said loudly, 'you got visitor.'

Bradman snorted. His mouth closed, and he licked his lips. Then his eyes fluttered and opened. He rubbed them with the backs of his hands.

'Hi, Delroy,' he said.

He sat up. He shook his head and panted, like someone emerging from a strenuous swim in the sea. Then he threw the cover back and put his feet on the floor. He was wearing his underpants and a T-shirt. His other clothes were on the floor at the side of the bed. Hurriedly he pulled them on.

'Does you want somet'in' to eat?' the woman asked.

'No,' said Bradman, 'I'll pick somet'in' up on the way.'

He pulled his tam over his uncombed hair and ran his hand over it to see that it was set right.

'Come on,' he said. 'Let's go.'

As Delroy left the room, he had a picture of the woman rocking in her chair to send the baby to sleep, and at the same time stretching her arm over the table and raising the cup of tea carefully to her lips so that it wouldn't spill.

Outside, Bradman said with enthusiasm, 'That was a great night.'

Delroy could imagine it. He envied Bradman the life he led. During the day, the flat was ghostly and still, full of the sound of sleepers. But at night, it was different. Delroy had spent evenings there when everything was quite changed. The place was full of activity, of comings and goings. It was full of the roaring voices and jokes of older men, of angry accusations over games of cards or dominoes that subsided as quickly as they had arisen with laughter and back-slapping. The smell of smoke filled the rooms. Meals were casually thrown together and eaten from plates balanced on laps. Fingers were used to strip chicken joints of their meat. Rice-and-peas were scooped up with bread. Cans were opened, bottles were emptied. When a glass fell and was broken, the pieces were kicked into a corner for someone else to clear up in the morning.

Bradman was accepted as a full member of this adult world. He used to stay up as late as his brothers — till two or three in the morning. His father and the woman he lived with — Bradman's mother had died when he was ten — didn't bother about him very much. He could please himself. Delroy envied him his freedom. It was so different from his own situation. He couldn't do anything without his parents getting at him. He couldn't go anywhere without them wanting to know where he was going. If he ever came back late, there was always a row.

Delroy told Bradman about the letter.

'What you worried 'bout?' asked Bradman. 'You've t'iefed letters before, 'aven't you?'

'Yes, I know,' said Delroy. 'But I always get found out.'

'I don' see why,' said Bradman. 'I t'ief 'em all the time an' nobody find out.'

'It's all right for you,' said Delroy. 'Your dad doesn't care if he gets letters or not from the school about you.'

'Yeah,' admitted Bradman, amused. 'I don' know why I bother to t'ief 'em anyway. 'E can't read what it say.'

'Whenever my dad gets a letter from school, he goes crazy, man.'

'Don' worry 'bout it. What it matter what 'e say?'

'It's all right for you,' repeated Delroy. 'You're not

31

there when he says it.'

'If I was,' said Bradman. 'I wouldn' put up wit' it. Who 'e think 'e is? Why you do what 'e tell you to?'

Bradman had said things like this before. It was easy for him to talk. He could do what he liked. His father didn't throw a tantrum every time something went wrong. Bradman could lead his own life. But for Delroy it was different. Bradman just didn't realize what his father was like. His every move was spied upon. Any whisper of complaint, and his father would shout and rave like a maniac. It was all very well for Bradman to tell Delroy to stand up for himself and do what he pleased. Bradman just didn't have any understanding of the kind of pressure Delroy was under.

Then Bradman had an idea.

'If they find out the school send a letter, you can always say it got lost in the post. Play it innocent. Play it cool. That's the best way.'

Delroy wasn't convinced. It seemed too easy. His father would never believe something like that. Letters did get lost in the post, but never letters from school complaining about Delroy's behaviour.

There was no point in going on to tell Bradman about the appointment his parents were supposed to make to see the headmaster and what would happen when his parents didn't telephone about it. It was all beyond Bradman's experience. His father never went to the school, and no one seemed to bother about it. But Delroy's father was different.

'Anyway, don' worry 'bout stupid letters,' said Bradman. 'I'm 'ungry. Let's go an' pick up some biscuits.'

And that, as far as Bradman was concerned, was the end of the letter.

They made their way to the shopping centre. There was an Asian grocer's there where, if you stood in a certain position, it was possible to slip a packet of biscuits into your bag without being seen by the cashier at her desk. This was where Bradman usually collected his breakfast.

SIX

At registration at the end of the day, Mrs Lasky reminded Delroy about his detention for being rude to Mr Frobisher.

He liked Mrs Lasky. She was young and small, and rather pretty, he thought, even if she was white. Sometimes she went on a bit, nagging them about their homework or telling them off for getting into trouble. But she always had a smile and a kind word for him. Even when he had done something wrong and she had to scold him, she still did it in a way that made him feel that she was on his side.

This time she stopped him as he was going out of the door and said, 'Really, Delroy, I'm ashamed of you. You're never rude to me. Why do you have to be rude to Mr Frobisher?'

Delroy could tell from the way she spoke that she disapproved of what he had done. But she was more disappointed than angry.

'It's just the way he goes on at me,' he said.

'That's too easy,' said Mrs Lasky. 'It's no good blaming other people. You've got to be responsible for yourself. You shouldn't let other people affect you like this. I know what a pleasant, likeable boy you are. It upsets me when I hear what some of the other teachers say about you. As far as they are concerned, you are disruptive and offensive — an absolute pain to have in a class. Why can't you show them the good side that you show me?'

'I don't know, miss,' said Delroy.

Why did she have to ask him questions like that which he couldn't answer? It just made him feel more miserable for letting her down.

'All right, then, Delroy,' sighed Mrs Lasky. 'You'd better go to your detention and get it over with.'

'Yes, miss.'

'And remember,' Mrs Lasky warned. 'No more trouble.'

33

'No, miss.'

They stared at each other for a moment, very seriously and solemnly. Then gradually their expressions relaxed, and they both found themselves smiling.

'Get along with you,' said Mrs Lasky, laughing. 'You'll be the death of me yet.'

With a cheeky grin, Delroy skipped out of the room.

As usual, boys on detention were waiting outside Room 3 for the class to be dismissed and the room to be available for their use. Bradman was among them.

'Let's go to McDonald's afterwards,' he suggested to Delroy.

'I've no money,' said Delroy.

'That's all right,' said Bradman. 'I'll pay.'

But it wasn't money that was worrying Delroy. He had suddenly remembered that he hadn't told his mother about the detention. Not that that would matter much. If he went straight home afterwards, he would arrive there at about his usual time.

Going to McDonald's was different. If he went there, he would be home late. Was it worth taking the risk? He still had the letter hanging over him. He didn't know what the outcome of that would be. He had destroyed the letter, but that wouldn't necessarily stop his parents from finding out. Then there would be trouble. Perhaps it wasn't worth taking the chance of more rows for being late as well.

'I'll think about it,' he told Bradman.

The teacher taking detention arrived. It was Miss Paxton, a new teacher with no sense of humour. Delroy had learned from experience that there was simply no point in making jokes with her. She just didn't take them in the right way. Flustered and red-cheeked, Miss Paxton ordered the boys into the classroom.

'Now, sit down quietly,' she said, 'and answer your names when I call them out.'

You could tell from her hot face and the untidy way in which her hair was disarrayed and stuck out that she had had a bad day. Her classes had been difficult and given her hell. As far as she was concerned, this additional chore of having to take detention was the final indignity. Delroy

34

toyed with the idea of increasing her burdens by playing the fool, but he decided against it. It wasn't worth it. There would be no fun in it. He would only get into trouble.

Miss Paxton issued each boy with a sheet of paper. She wrote the word 'Disestablishmentarianism' on the board.

'Now,' she announced, 'I want you to make up as many different words as possible using only the letters contained in the word.'

'Please, miss,' began one boy, 'what does it mean?'

'That's not important,' replied Miss Paxton.

'Can we use the same letter twice?' asked another boy.

'Only if the letter appears twice in the word.'

'Can we use two-letter words?' asked a third boy.

'Yes,' said Miss Paxton. 'That's permissible.'

'What about four-letter words?' asked the first boy, trying to look innocent.

'Just you get on with it quietly,' said Miss Paxton, sensing that the boy was being awkward. 'Never mind all these questions. You know what to do. Now do it.'

Delroy mumbled resentfully to himself beneath his breath. What a stupid way to spend his time. What a stupid word. What did it mean anyway? Was there such a word? Half-heartedly he began to write down words made up from the various letters:

> table
> stable
> dish
> establish
> blame
> stare

They were obvious.

Then he found a couple of more difficult words:

> disaster
> blemish

before boredom set in again.

Indignation began to well up in him. It wasn't fair that he should be sitting there wasting his time just because of Mr Frobisher. If Mr Frobisher had only been more reasonable, none of this would have happened — the detention, the letter, the worry about what would happen if his father found out about it all. He still couldn't see why it was his job to pick paper up from the floor. He hadn't put it there. It was just like teachers.

But then gloom swept over him again. What did it matter anyway? He was here in the detention room now, and there was nothing he could do about it other than endure it.

He began to look for words that fitted his jaundiced mood. There were a number of them. He found and wrote down:

> stab
>
> tear
>
> detest
>
> hate

Suddenly he discovered exactly the right word. He put his hand on his head and rubbed his hair backwards and forwards in triumph. He checked again to make sure. Yes, the word was there. He hadn't imagined it. He wrote it down:

> shit

No other word could sum up Delroy's feelings about the detention. It was perfect.

He was exultant. It was too good to keep to himself. He leaned over to Bradman who was sitting beside him and showed him the word gleefully. His friend stared at it in disbelief and then let out a whoop of delighted shock that had every head in the room turning in his direction.

Miss Paxton's hot and apprehensive face glared at him. 'What are you laughing at?' she demanded.

'Nothing, miss,' mumbled Bradman.

Miss Paxton came and stood in front of them. She took up Bradman's paper and read through the words. Then she looked at Delroy's. When her eyes reached the improper word, her lips tightened.

'I shall speak to your form teacher about you tomorrow,' she said.

'Why?' asked Delroy belligerently.

'You know perfectly well why,' returned Miss Paxton.

'No I don't.'

'Oh, yes you do. Because of that word you've written down.'

36

'What word?' challenged Delroy, hoping that Miss Paxton would say it out loud.

'You know quite well what word,' said Miss Paxton coolly.

'All the letters are there,' protested Delroy. 'It's a perfectly fair word according to the rules.'

'You know we don't allow words like that,' said Miss Paxton.

She turned on the other boys who were standing up, straining on tiptoe and craning their necks to get a view of the word that was arousing so much comment.

'Get back to your work, all of you,' she practically screamed at them, a feeling of hysteria getting the better of her.

The boys scuttled back to their places. Miss Paxton took the offending sheet away and brought another piece of paper for Delroy to start again.

'It's not fair,' said Delroy. 'I was only following the rules.'

'Start again,' said Miss Paxton.

'Cha!' snarled Delroy contemptuously, and he sat for the rest of the detention sullenly staring at the blank sheet of paper.

It was typical of teachers, he thought. They made rules, and then when you kept to them, they changed the rules. Anything to get you into trouble.

It was the same with parents. They made their rules too — only their rules were so impossible that you couldn't help breaking them. They seemed to be made with the deliberate intention of tricking their children into breaking them. Then the parents had an excuse for punishing the children. All the power was loaded on one side. Children didn't stand a chance.

In spite of some pointed looks from Miss Paxton, which Delroy saw but ignored, he spent the rest of the hour absorbed in his gloomy reflections. He did not write a single word.

At last the hour was over, and Delroy was free to go. As he walked up to Miss Paxton's desk to hand in his sheet, he fixed his eyes on her threateningly, daring her to make some comment. He was sure she had noticed that he had done no work. But she carefully kept her gaze away from his and busied herself with stacking the sheets of paper into a neat pile.

Delroy felt cheated. Miss Paxton was useless. You couldn't even have a real row with her.

Bradman was waiting for him outside the classroom.

'Are you comin'?' he asked Delroy eagerly.

'I suppose so,' replied Delroy. The answer came without thought. He presumed the decision had been there all the time without his knowing it—though even as he spoke the words he wasn't sure that it was really what he wanted.

Once announced, however, there was no doubt in his mind. Yes, he would go to McDonald's. Why shouldn't he? Why shouldn't he have some fun? Why shouldn't he enjoy himself? If his parents were angry with him for staying out late, that was too bad. He had a right to lead his own life. If his parents didn't like it, they knew what they could do.

'Great, man, great,' rejoiced Bradman.

'I ain't got no money,' reminded Delroy.

'That's all right,' said Bradman magnanimously. 'I can pay.'

As usual, Delroy knew better than to ask his friend where he had got the money from. If Bradman was ever short of money, he always knew how to get some.

SEVEN

McDonald's was a popular hang-out place for young, black kids. If you stayed long enough, so the rumours went, you would see a knife fight. There were one or two older boys there when Delroy and Bradman arrived, but there wasn't a knife in sight.

'Well, if it isn't Bradman,' said the black assistant behind the counter. He wasn't much older than Bradman himself. 'Somebody told me you'd gone to detention centre.'

38

'They're not fast enough to catch me,' said Bradman smugly.

'Don't say that too often,' warned the assistant. 'One of these days, you're going to trip over their fat feet.'

Bradman bought Delroy a beefburger, and they stood by the window eating them. Outside, they could see a group of black boys loitering and passing the time of day. Whenever a girl walked by, they became alert and drew themselves up. Comments were bandied about. The girls looked in their direction and then hurried on. The boys slumped to their former lazy poses.

'Not much happ'nin' tonight,' said Bradman. 'This is dread. Let's go to the Paradise.'

Delroy began to worry about arriving home late. If he went now, he would be late, but not too late. He could invent some kind of excuse. If he went to the Paradise, no excuse would be possible. But Bradman had bought him a beefburger. To leave him now would seem a very mean desertion. He would have to risk being late.

'Right,' he said.

The Birds of Paradise was a youth club. There was nothing in the rules and regulations to say that it was a youth club for black boys and girls, but that is more or less what it amounted to. There were only ever one or two white faces to be seen there.

It had an exciting atmosphere, for though nothing dangerous was going on, it seemed that something unusual or violent might happen at any moment. There was electricity in the air. At the same time, it was relaxed. Delroy and Bradman felt they could be themselves. There was no one spying on them or waiting to pounce on them if they said the wrong word or did the wrong thing.

It all had something to do with the noise and the lights. A reggae record was blaring out of the loudspeaker making conversation practically impossible. Not that anyone worried about that. They hadn't come here to talk. The fluorescent lighting gave everything a bright, unreal glow. Although it was still early in the evening, there was a lot going on. At one end of the hall, boys were playing table-tennis. In the middle, there was a crowd around the two snooker tables. A queue was already forming at the bar. Bradman and Delroy had to wait.

When their turn came, Bradman bought his friend a Coke and offered him a cigarette. Ant'ny came over to them.

'I've booked a table,' he announced. 'D'you fancy a game?'

Bradman and Delroy took it in turns to play table-tennis against Ant'ny. It was hot in the youth club, and they were soon sweating. Standing legs astride, his eyes concentrating fiercely on the ball, his arm shooting out to slice it back to Ant'ny's side of the table, Delroy felt all his faculties in action. He was alive and alert in a way that he never was at school or at home.

Bradman lost his game, but Delroy won. It gave him a tremendous sense of exhilaration to be the victor.

'It was luck, man, luck,' said Ant'ny. 'That's all there was to it.'

'Oh no, it wasn't,' said Delroy. 'You don't know skill when you see it.'

'Was that skill?' asked Ant'ny, looking round at his friends in disbelief. 'Was that skill? I didn' see no skill.'

'How else you lose then?' asked Delroy.

'It's early in the ev'nin',' explained Ant'ny. 'I don' 'ave my eye in yet.'

'Ah, go back to you tree 'ouse,' said Bradman contemptuously.

'Yeah, go back to you banana house,' added Delroy.

Ant'ny was well known for being a bad loser, but not even his grumbles and excuses could spoil Delroy's sense of his own achievement. The only thought that disturbed his high spirits was what might be waiting for him at home when he arrived. He decided it was time to leave.

'I'm off then,' he said.

'But the ev'nin' jus' beginnin',' complained Bradman.

'I'll get into trouble if I'm late,' Delroy explained.

'Who's a mummy's boy then?' jeered Ant'ny.

'Please yourself,' said Bradman.

Delroy hesitated. He would much prefer to stay here with his friends, here at the Paradise with its music and lights, and the feeling that something might happen at any moment. All right, nothing very much was actually going on, but any minute now. . . . It was life — his life, and the life of his friends. Why did he have to miss all the fun?

He turned to Bradman, wanting to explain all this to him, seeking his support to strengthen his growing resolve to defy his parents.

But Bradman was preparing to face Ant'ny again. He had already forgotten about Delroy.

EIGHT

All the way home Delroy worried about what he was going to find there and what he was going to say. He knew his mother would be anxious about him. She would have been expecting him home at his usual time after school. And then there was his father. He would be sure to make a scene.

It was not as though he was all that late. He needn't say where he had been. He could say he had gone round to Bradman's. It was near enough the truth.

It had started to rain. The heavy drizzle made Delroy shiver. He huddled more deeply inside his anorak and put the hood up to try and keep warm and dry. It wasn't far now.

As he turned the corner into his street, he examined the cars parked along the kerbside. He always did this to see whether his father's car was there or not. Then he had a better idea of what to expect and how to prepare himself. He looked up and down the street. His father's car wasn't there. Perhaps luck was going to be on his side after all.

As he let himself in at the front door, his mother came into the hall.

'Where have you been?' she demanded. 'I've been worried sick wondering what had happened to you.'

Delroy noticed that his mother looked tired. There were deep rings under her eyes, and her eyes moved restlessly, not still for a single moment. She made a show of being angry and annoyed, but somehow it rang false. Delroy knew that her mind was elsewhere.

'I've been round at Bradman's,' he said in excuse.

'You know your father said you weren't to mix with him anymore.'

'He's a friend,' said Delroy. 'I can't help it.'

'Your father also told you to come straight home after school,' continued Mrs Ellis reproachfully. 'You could at least have told me you were going to be late.'

'I didn't know,' Delroy muttered. 'It just happened.'

Mrs Ellis noticed how damp Delroy's clothes were. She ran her hands over his arms and shoulders.

'You're soaking wet,' she cried.

Delroy began to shiver again. Outside he had been aware of the chill and the rain, but it was only now in the warmth of the house that he fully realized how cold he was.

'Take that wet thing off,' said Mrs Ellis. She started to unzip his anorak and pull it off him. 'Go in there and get warm while I find you something to eat.'

Delroy went into the front room and sat in front of the electric fire. The television was on, the volume turned down so that the sound came over as a faint background. Barry was sitting at the table doing his homework.

'Where have you been?' he asked. 'Dad won't half be mad.'

'Shut your mouth,' responded Delroy.

Barry pulled a face at his brother expressing contempt and indifference and went back to his writing.

Delroy felt the front half of his body begin to heat up. His trousers started to stiffen. Clouds of steam rose from them as they became hot and the dampness was driven out. He turned round so that the same thing could happen to the back. His mother came in with a mug of soup.

'Here,' she said, 'start with that.'

Delroy cupped the mug in his hands. The soup was so hot he could only take tiny sips from it. Gradually, the liquid spread through his body, the warmth returning.

His mother came in again, this time carrying a plate of beefburgers and beans. Delroy didn't like to say that he

42

had already eaten that evening—and a beefburger as well. Anyway, he was hungry again, and he wasn't the kind of boy to turn down the offer of food.

'Now clear the table, Barry,' said Mrs Ellis.

Barry pulled a face again and began to gather his papers together so that there was room for his brother. Delroy sat down and started to eat. He wolfed down the food, emptying the plate in minutes.

'Barry,' said his mother, 'it's time you were in bed.'

'But I haven't finished my homework yet,' objected Barry.

'I don't care,' said Mrs Ellis. 'I don't want any arguments.'

Barry made a great fuss of collecting his books and papers together and putting them in his bag before going out. It was his way of registering his protest.

Mrs Ellis came and sat in the seat Barry had vacated. Delroy looked at his empty plate. He waited for the moral chat that he knew was coming.

'I don't know what your father is going to say when he gets in,' said Mrs Ellis.

Delroy nearly said that he could imagine only too clearly what his father would say, but he kept quiet.

'You mustn't think he's being hard on you,' continued Mrs Ellis. 'He gets angry because he's worried about you. He's concerned about you. He doesn't want you to get into trouble.'

Delroy was not convinced. What he felt was that his father couldn't be bothered with him any more. He had had enough. Delroy felt the same. A state of stalemate had been reached. If his father couldn't be bothered with Delroy, then Delroy couldn't be bothered with his father.

But he didn't put this into words. He knew his mother was only trying to help. She was trying to be sympathetic and understand. She was on his side.

'He doesn't have to know, does he?' he asked hopefully, raising his eyes to look at his mother. Even if he didn't care what his father said or did, it was always better to avoid a scene if he could.

'It's not as easy as that,' said Mrs Ellis.

43

For a moment, her eyes became vacant. It was as though she had forgotten the present and was watching a private film going on in her mind. Then she shook herself back to consciousness.

'All right,' she said. 'I'll try to sort it out. But I can't go on taking your side against your father. I've got a marriage to keep up, and I've got to think of that as well. The two of you are pulling me apart.'

Delroy didn't really understand what she meant. All he knew was that he was safe — at least for the moment. His mother would keep quiet about his late arrival home. She would see that everything was all right.

'Now you'd better go to bed,' Mrs Ellis said.

She stretched out her hand and placed it on Delroy's head, her palm pressing against his springy hair and pushing his head down. Delroy allowed his head to go with the pressure at first, and then reared back against it. His mother's hand grasped his skull and shook it, and she laughed. Delroy found himself smiling.

'Off you go then,' she said as she rose. She pulled Delroy to his feet and directed him towards the door.

As he was going out, Delroy turned to face his mother.

'Thanks, Mum,' he said.

NINE

There was basketball practice after school the next evening. Delroy was looking forward to it. He was feeling more cheerful. There had been no mention of the letter either at home or at school. Perhaps he was going to get away with it after all.

He hurried down to the changing room and put on his practice kit. Then he bounded into the gym.

Most of the other members of the squad were already there. The boom of balls bouncing against the wooden floor thundered in the air. Leaping figures attacked the baskets at both ends of the gym. Balls soared through the air and dropped into the baskets, or hit the edge and ricochetted off. Sometimes they spun round the rim of the basket, holding the thrower in agonised suspense before finally falling through or being disappointingly rejected.

Delroy retrieved a loose ball. The roundness and heaviness of it in his hands was satisfying. He bounced it a couple of times on the spot to get the feel of it, before propelling it in front of him to the other end of the gym. He steadied himself. He balanced the ball in his hands. He reared up with it towards the basket. With a sharp flick of his wrist he urged the ball into the air. It dropped down true and dead straight through the centre of the basket. It was a great feeling.

Mr Miller, the teacher in charge of the team, called the boys together. Abandoned balls thumped themselves to a standstill.

Delroy listened attentively to what Mr Miller had to say. He liked Mr Miller. He spoke to you like an equal. He was always ready to hear your side of the story.

'Now, we've got an important match next week,' Mr Miller was saying. 'The cup match against Northlands. They've got a strong side. They beat us last year in the cup. But that's no reason why they should beat us this time. What we need is a bit of discipline — keeping your eye on the ball all the time and not going to sleep. We can do it. We've got the potential. If only we can get it all together.'

It was one of Mr Miller's favourite expressions. He was always urging his team to 'get it all together'.

They began with some exercises. In pairs, they ran the length of the gym, passing the ball to each other. Then they took it in turns to bounce the ball down the gym while the partner moved backwards trying to block the ball or take possession.

Delroy was matched against Stephen. He watched the frown of concentration on the captain's face. Stephen took it all very seriously. His eyes were alert, darting everywhere. You could almost see him thinking. Delroy wished that he could concentrate as hard as that — shut everything else out, bring all his energy and intellect to bear on the one important thing of the moment: passing the ball accurately, getting past your man, putting the ball in the basket.

All the time Mr Miller was shouting at them — urging them on, praising them, correcting them, giving advice.

Before long, Delroy was panting. He had to wipe the sweat out of his eyes. It was a good feeling. It was as though all the stale air was being pumped out of his lungs and being replaced by fresh air; as though all his pores were being washed clean.

After some more exercises, the boys were split into two teams and played a session. It began slowly with fumbles and dropped balls and unsuccessful baskets. Then the players got into their stride. They established a rhythm. The pace started to heat up. The ball was driven from one end of the gym to the other. Each side in turn scored basket after basket. The speed of the play was so fast that Delroy could hardly keep up. He could feel his vest sticking to his back. No sooner had he chased down to one end of the gym than he was forced to race after the ball to the other end. When the whistle finally came, all the boys were exhausted. But they were also high. It had been exciting. They had really pushed themselves.

'Great!' cried Mr Miller. 'You show that form next week, and Northlands had better look out.'

Back in the changing room the boys were full of themselves. Delroy sat, in total collapse, on the bench breathing heavily, his legs stretched out, a broad smile on his face. He listened to the others congratulating their friends on baskets they had scored or prevented. A sense of happy contentment flowed through his weary body.

Afterwards Delroy walked part of the way home with Stephen. He had always been rather wary of Stephen in the past. He regarded him as something of a teachers' pet. Stephen never spoke out of turn in class. He kept himself to himself during breaks. He always did his homework. He actually seemed to be interested in the work. Delroy couldn't think of a single occasion when a teacher had had a bad word to say about him. He felt that Stephen wasn't quite normal. Not that he would have dared say it to his face. Stephen was a big boy. No one picked a quarrel with Stephen.

There was another thing. Stephen was never seen out

at night. He never went to the Paradise or to McDonald's or anywhere. He never hung around the shopping centre waiting for something to happen. He always went straight home after school and stayed there.

During the silence which followed excited chat about the practice, Delroy decided to raise the subject with Stephen.

'How come you're never down the Paradise?' he asked.

'My parents won't let me,' explained Stephen. There was no regret in his voice. It was simply a statement of fact.

'That's grim, man,' said Delroy.

'It's not important,' said Stephen. 'I don't particularly want to go.' He wasn't putting on an act, Delroy was sure. He meant it. 'I've got so much else to do.'

'You mean your homework,' said Delroy, coming as close to a sneer as he dared.

'Yes, that and other things.'

'I don't know how you can stand to stay in every night and do your homework.'

'I don't see anything wrong in wanting to get on,' said Stephen. 'I want to be a journalist, and to be any good you have to have your A levels at least, or go to a university. University is probably better. Then you can start nearer the top. You might start with a national paper instead of just a local rag.'

Delroy listened amazed and not a little awed. Stephen had it all worked out. A Levels. University. That was three or six years ahead. Delroy had no idea what he would be doing then. He couldn't think that far into the future. He couldn't be sure he would still be alive!

Then Delroy remembered something else he had heard about Stephen. His father was a minister, wasn't he?

'Is it true that you go to church three times every Sunday?' he asked.

'Usually,' replied Stephen. 'So what?'

'Nothing,' said Delroy, still slightly mocking. 'I just wondered.'

'It's as good a place as any if you want to think,' said Stephen. 'You should try it some time.'

Delroy couldn't help admiring Stephen's self-suffici-
ency. There was no rattling him. He knew what he wanted
and was set on getting it. He didn't care what other people
thought.

Delroy felt a touch of envy. His other friends sometimes made fun of Stephen among themselves or even
indirectly to his face. But it didn't seem to make any
difference to Stephen. He didn't get angry or upset. He kept
even-tempered, laughed about it pleasantly, and went on
ploughing his own furrow. Yes, Delroy couldn't help envy-
ing him.

TEN

When Delroy arrived home, his mother was waiting for
him. Usually, she was in the kitchen or busy upstairs, but
today as he opened the door, she came into the hall to meet
him. He sensed at once from the way she looked at him
that something was wrong. He knew he was late. He realized he had forgotten to tell her about the basketball
practice. Was that what it was?

'Come in here,' Mrs Ellis said. 'I want to talk to you.'

They went into the front room. Delroy sat down
uncomfortably. His mother's voice was cold. He feared the
worst.

'I had a 'phone call at work today from the school,' Mrs
Ellis began.

Delroy bowed his head. He didn't dare look at her.

'Mrs Lasky said you had been in some trouble there.
She also said the school had written a letter about it. She
was surprised that I hadn't contacted her.'

Delroy didn't dare raise his head.

'What's all this about?' Mrs Ellis demanded. 'What
was in that letter, and where is it?'

'I don't know,' said Delroy. He remembered Bradman's suggestion. 'Perhaps it's been lost in the post.'

Now he tried looking at his mother. Her gaze was
unflinching. She wasn't having any of that.

'It wouldn't be the first time you've stolen a letter so

48

that we wouldn't find out about you,' she continued. 'And you know what happened then.'

Yes, Delroy did. His father had beaten him.

'Oh, it's nothing, Mum,' said Delroy, this time evading the issue. 'It's just some trouble with one of the teachers. He's always picking on me.'

'From what Mrs Lasky said, it seems more as though you're picking on him. I've told you, Delroy, about being cheeky to teachers. You've got to show them the same respect you show us. They're there to help you. If you mess about all the time, you're not going to make any progress or get anywhere.'

She went and sat beside Delroy on the sofa. She put her arm around him. Delroy still avoided looking at her.

'Why can't you keep out of trouble?' she pleaded. 'You know how it upsets me. I've got my job to do all day. I've got to come home and look after you and Barry. And then there's your father. He's started. . . .'

She stopped and didn't continue what she was going to say.

'I've got enough worries without you adding to them all the time by getting into trouble,' she said instead.

Delroy stared miserably at his shoes.

'I don't mean to get into trouble,' he mumbled.

'You don't mean to, you don't mean to!' repeated Mrs Ellis impatiently. She got up and began walking about the room. 'Why don't you do something about it then? You're big enough now to know what's right and what's wrong. You ought to be able to look after yourself. Sometimes I don't think you want to do the right things.'

'I can't help it,' said Delroy looking at her for sympathy.

'Of course you can help it,' said Mrs Ellis turning on him. 'You just don't try. I'll have to tell your father this time. I've kept things quiet before in the hope that you would come to your senses, but I can't keep going on hiding things from him. He's your father, and he ought to know about it.'

Delroy's face clouded over, and he scowled at his mother.

'And you needn't look at me like that. You've got nobody to blame but yourself. The best thing would be for you to be in bed when your father comes in. Then I can try to find the most suitable moment to tell him. That's the best I can do for you.' Her tone was grudging. 'But I can't go on protecting you all the time. You've got to stand on your own feet, and be responsible for your own behaviour.'

Delroy was confused. It was just like adults. They wanted you to obey their rules, and at the same time they expected you to be responsible for yourself. They couldn't have it both ways. What they meant was that they wanted you to be responsible for yourself by obeying their rules. You couldn't make the rules for yourself. That wasn't allowed.

If only he could be like Bradman. Bradman could do what he liked. His father didn't care what he did. He could stay out late if he wanted to. He could stay out all night. He could get into any kind of trouble, and his father didn't bother.

Or if he could be like Stephen. Stephen had no difficulty doing what his parents required him to do. He stayed at home. He did his homework. He went to church. He even seemed to enjoy obeying the rules.

With Delroy it was different. He wanted to lead his own life like Bradman. And yet oddly, at the same time, he wanted to obey the rules like Stephen. The only thing was that it wasn't possible to do both. When he did what he wanted to do, it always ended in trouble. When he tried to follow the rules, he always failed.

He didn't enjoy getting into trouble. He resented being criticized and told off. He answered back. And so he got into more trouble. It was like being trapped in a deep pit of mud. The more he kicked against it and tried to get out, the deeper he sank into the mud, and the harder it was to escape. There were times when he felt that he would be swallowed up completely and that would be the end of it.

He knew that his mother did try to understand. She did try to help. But it wasn't enough. He still got into trouble. He knew that she was right. The only person who could really help him was himself.

He recalled what his mother had said. He had to stand on his own feet. He had to be responsible for his own behaviour.

'I'll try, Mum,' he said.

ELEVEN

Hostile voices woke Delroy that night. Rising from the submerged depths of sleep, he heard the angry words booming in the room below. He buried his head under the bedclothes, but it was no use. The voices went on clanging in his head. He threw the covers back and lay there for a moment trying to make out the words. Then he got out of bed. He groped his way to the door and opened it. The light was still on in the hall downstairs. He tiptoed slowly down, remembering that the second step from the top creaked.

The voices became louder and more distinct. His mother and father were having a row.

'I know you've been with a woman,' his mother was shouting. 'I can smell her on you. You disgust me.'

'Don't talk stupid, woman,' came his father's voice. 'I've been working late.'

'Working late — that's all you ever do,' jeered Mrs Ellis.

'Well, somebody's got to bring some money in.'

'What do you mean? I work, too, in case you've forgotten. And I bring up the children.'

'That's your job, woman.'

'Yes, yes, yes,' said Mrs Ellis. 'That's fine for you, isn't it? You go out enjoying yourself while I'm stuck here, looking after the children and coping with their problems.'

'Is Delroy in trouble again then?' asked Mr Ellis sharply.

'No.' Mrs Ellis's voice faltered. 'No, I don't think so.'

'Did he come home straight after school today?'

'Yes.'

'I don't know what you're arguing about then.'

51

'I'm arguing about you being out night after night with some fancy woman,' said Mrs Ellis coming back to the attack.

'Oh, don't go on about that again,' said Mr Ellis wearily.

'It's true though, isn't it?'

The voices went on. They would go on for some time longer.

Delroy climbed the stairs again to his bedroom. He jumped into bed and curled himself into a ball, shivering a little from the cold air on the stairs. He pulled the bedclothes up over his ears to muffle the angry words from below, and tried to go to sleep.

TWELVE

Delroy sat outside the headmaster's room waiting for his parents to arrive. Of course his mother had had to tell his father about the trouble with Mr Frobisher. They had had to make an appointment to see Mr Johnson. But she had been as good as her word. She had chosen her moment. Mr Ellis had been annoyed, but no more annoyed than usual. He had had a go at Delroy, telling him that he was tired of him getting into trouble. He was tired of having to take time off work and having to go up to the school to sort things out. But he left it at that.

There had been no mention of the letter. His mother had covered up for him — again. There was a possibility that Mr Johnson would refer to it when he saw Delroy's parents. Then there would be another row. Delroy prayed that that wouldn't happen.

'Don't look so worried,' said a voice.

Delroy looked up. It was Mrs Lasky. His face brightened when he saw her.

'That's better,' she said. 'Have your parents arrived yet?'

'No, miss,' said Delroy.

'I'll come back when they're here then. And remember to smile. It's not as bad as all that.'

Delroy did as he was told. It was easy to smile for somebody like Mrs Lasky. Why was that, he wondered? If Mr Frobisher had asked him to smile, he'd have told him to get lost. But then Mr Frobisher never would ask him to smile.

He hoped Mr Frobisher wasn't going to be present at the interview with his parents. That would be too much. He wasn't sure if he would be able to stand it if Mr Frobisher was there.

By this time the smile had faded from Delroy's face. When his parents arrived he felt as depressed as ever. He didn't look at his parents, but he was very conscious of his father scowling at him.

Mrs Lasky returned, and they all went into the headmaster's office. It was a small room, and with five of them, it seemed very crowded. Mr Johnson shook hands with Mr and Mrs Ellis. His mother gave a nervous smile, but she seemed subdued and worried. His father was suddenly all grins and affability. He always put on a performance like this, Delroy thought. Nobody knew what his father was really like — except him.

They sat down leaving Delroy standing in the middle of the floor. He felt conspicuous and embarrassed. His head drooped and he put his hands behind his back. It was just like being on trial.

'Sit down, Delroy,' said Mr Johnson, indicating a seat in the corner.

Then Mr Johnson turned to Mr and Mrs Ellis.

'Thank you very much for coming up to school,' he said. 'I know it's not always convenient, and you have to take time off work, but I think it's useful to have a talk about Delroy and his behaviour. It's not just the incident with Mr Frobisher. But we can begin with that. I think I told you in my letter. . . .'

Delroy hadn't really been listening to Mr Johnson droning on, but at the word 'letter', he was instantly alert.

'What letter?' asked Mr Ellis. The smile had gone from his face. 'I don't know anything about any letter.'

'I told you about it,' said Mrs Ellis quickly. 'I told you what was in it,' she amended.

Mr Ellis let it pass, but there was an ominous look on his face.

'Anyway,' said Mr Johnson, resuming his speech, 'there have been other bits of trouble. Oh, nothing very serious. He's been rude to some other teachers. He's late for lessons and late in the morning. He keeps getting detentions for not doing his homework. He's been caught smoking. That sort of thing. And they've been mounting up.'

Delroy felt his father's eyes burning a hole right through his head. He didn't dare look up.

'The thing is,' went on Mr Johnson, 'Delroy is a bright boy. He's got potential. But at the moment he's just wasting it all.'

Mrs Lasky came in. 'I put round a work report on Delroy. Nearly all the teachers say he's got ability, but he doesn't use it. He could do really well in his exams if he wanted to. And then he could go on to the sixth form and to college or university even.'

Delroy was surprised to hear this. It was the first time anyone had mentioned college or university to him. Teachers in the past had told him that he was bright, but he didn't know how bright. He knew he could get by in class without bothering very much. He could do enough to satisfy the teachers with only half of his mind. Perhaps that was part of the trouble.

'Yes, I know,' his mother was saying. 'But what can we do about it?'

'For a start,' asked Mr Johnson, 'how much homework does he do?'

'I never see him doing any,' said Mr Ellis.

'He goes to his room every night to get on with it,' said Mrs Ellis.

'All he does is play that blasted record-player,' said Mr Ellis.

'Do you ever look at the work he does?' asked Mr Johnson.

'Yes, sometimes,' said Mrs Ellis.

'He never seems to bring any books home,' said Mr Ellis.

How would he know, thought Delroy bitterly. How

would he know whether he did any homework or whether he had any books. He was hardly ever home in the evenings anyway, and when he was, Delroy might as well be part of the furniture for all the notice he took of him. His father just ignored him.

'Then there are his friends,' continued Mr Johnson. 'He doesn't exactly pick the best people to go around with. That's part of the reason why he gets into the kind of trouble he does get into.'

'I know the friends you mean,' said Mrs Ellis.

'They're bad boys,' said Mr Ellis. 'He's out with them at night till all hours.'

'That's where the danger is,' said Mr Johnson. 'If he's roaming the streets with his friends, he's likely to get into trouble. I wouldn't want to see Delroy picked up by the police.'

Delroy remembered the policeman in the shopping centre pushing him into the panda car and insulting him. What could Mr Johnson know about a thing like that? He couldn't know that you didn't have to do anything to be picked up by the police if you were black.

'I just don't understand it,' said Mr Ellis despairingly. 'We work hard to give him a good home. He's got everything he wants. If there is anything he needs, he has only to ask for it. And then he lets us down like this. He's a bad boy. That's all there is about it.'

'I don't think so,' said Mrs Lasky. 'There's a very nice side to Delroy. He's just going through a difficult patch at the moment, and we've got to try to see him through. In a couple of years' time you'll be surprised at what a fine young man he's turned out to be.'

'I hope so,' said Mrs Ellis, but from her tone she didn't sound very certain.

'Why can't he be like Barry?' asked Mr Ellis. 'He never gets into the kind of trouble Delroy gets into. He's a great kid.'

Delroy saw that his father was smiling again.

'Well, yes,' agreed Mr Johnson grudgingly. 'But there's a naughty side to Barry, too.'

'Yes, but he's clever with it,' said Mr Ellis. He

chuckled admiringly and approvingly. 'He knows how to get away with it. And he's in the football team, too. He's a great player.'

'Delroy's not so bad himself,' said Mrs Lasky. 'He plays basketball for the school.'

'Does he?' said Mr Ellis. 'Perhaps that's the trouble. Perhaps he spends too much time on his basketball and not enough on school work.'

'Oh, I think Delroy can do both,' said Mrs Lasky, 'if he puts his mind to it.'

'That's the problem,' said Mr Johnson. 'How do we get Delroy to do it?'

There was silence. Delroy looked up. All eyes were fixed on him. For the last quarter of an hour, they had been talking about him as if he weren't there. Now they expected him to say something. But what? He didn't know what they wanted to hear. It was strange. He could talk to Mr Johnson or to Mrs Lasky on his own without any bother, but with his parents there, he couldn't find the right words.

'Well, Delroy,' coaxed Mr Johnson. 'What's the answer?'

'I don't know,' mumbled Delroy.

'I think you do,' said Mr Johnson.

Delroy shrugged his shoulders and gritted his teeth. It was embarrassing. He would have to say something.

'I'll have to try harder,' he managed to bring out. 'I'll have to keep out of trouble.'

That seemed to be satisfactory.

'We'll have to keep our fingers crossed and hope he can do it,' said Mr Johnson.

He stood up.

'Let's leave it there, shall we?'

He came round to the front of his desk to join Mr and Mrs Ellis.

'Perhaps you can have a word with him tonight about it.'

'Yes,' said Mr Ellis. 'I'll talk to him all right.'

Delroy didn't like the sound of that.

THIRTEEN

For the rest of the day Delroy tried to behave himself. It wasn't too difficult. He had a double period with Mr Andrews. There was only Paul in the class to distract him. Then there was a double period of English with Mrs Lasky. He enjoyed English, and Mrs Lasky was a good teacher. So there were no problems there.

As usual, after school, he waited for his friends at the gate. Bradman came bounding down towards him.

'Hey,' he said, 'you 'eard that latest number by the Jumbies?'

'Sure,' said Delroy. 'It's great.'

'Yeah,' said Bradman. 'Let's not wait for the others. They've probably got detention anyway. I want to go an' get the disc.'

They set off down the road. Bradman began to sing the words of the song, imitating the weird, falsetto sound for which the Jumbies were famous. Delroy joined in.

Their walk turned into a dance as their bodies moved to the rhythm of the music. They patterned their steps over the whole width of the pavement, veering from side to side as they made their advance. An old woman with a shopping trolley stopped in their path. Her white face was open-mouthed with astonishment. She didn't know which way to move.

Still singing and dancing, Delroy and Bradman passed one on each side of her. When he looked back, Delroy saw that the old lady was still stationary. She was staring after them and muttering something. It just made him sing louder.

There was a large W.H. Smith's in the shopping centre, and Bradman hurried straight for it. Inside, Delroy was surprised that Bradman didn't automatically go to the record department. Instead, he wandered about idly, looking at the magazines and paperbacks and the displays of pens and stationery.

Eventually, they reached the record section. Bradman flipped through rack after rack of LPs, giving a good imitation of someone searching for a particularly rare record and determined not to give up until he had scrutinized every LP in the shop. Then he moved over to where the singles were on display. It was only then that the realization dawned upon Delroy that Bradman had no intention of buying the disc he wanted.

Delroy went hot all over. He looked quickly around him to see where the assistants were. He saw his reflection caught in a mirror positioned at an angle in the corner where the walls joined the ceiling. There was no one else near them. The assistant behind the counter was busy checking off a box of records against an order form. Nevertheless, Delroy felt as though all the oxygen had been sucked out of the shop: he couldn't breathe.

Bradman went on calmly examining the records, lifting them out one by one and twisting his head round to read the labels. It seemed almost by accident that first one record and then a second were slipped into the bag hanging from his shoulder instead of being replaced on the rack.

He went on meticulously picking records up, studying the labels and putting them back. At last he came to the final one. His mouth pouted as though in disappointment.

All Delroy wanted to do was to get out of the store as far as possible, but Bradman behaved as though he had all the time in the world. He went over to the magazines again. He took up a Kung Fu comic and began to leaf through it. Delroy could only stand beside him, desperately trying to conceal the agitation which shook his body.

'I 'aven't got this one,' said Bradman casually. 'It looks good.'

He carried it over to the cash desk and paid for it. Then he walked out of the store with Delroy following closely at his heels. When they were outside, Delroy still expected some hand to grab him by the shoulder and haul him in front of the manager, or some voice to call after them, 'Stop thief! Call the police!' He looked back towards the shop still fearful of pursuit. Delroy couldn't decide whether Bradman was an idiot for taking such risks or quite brilliant for carrying out the theft with such cool-ness.

'Crazy, man,' he said at last. 'You could have been caught.'

Stealing a bar of chocolate from a small newsagent's was one thing. They all did that. But lifting records from a big store like Smith's was something else. They probably had detectives there on the look-out for shoplifters. They would take anyone caught to court.

'Don't get excited,' said Bradman. 'You can get away wit' anyt'in if you keep calm enough. Nobody's goin' to miss a couple o' discs.'

'But supposing somebody had seen you,' went on Delroy. 'Supposing somebody had called the police.'

'There's always some way out,' said Bradman. 'Make a run for it, or swear blind you don' know what they talkin' 'bout.'

'I couldn't have done it,' said Delroy.

'Why not?' asked Bradman.

'I just wouldn't have the nerve.'

'Then you're a fool. Take what you can when you can. That's my motto. Nobody goin' to give you anyt'in'. You've got to take it.'

'What if you get caught and arrested?'

'That's not important. My brothers 'ave been in an' out o' court an' prison so often it's like a second 'ome to 'em. An' they still manage to 'ave some fun out o' life.'

Delroy wasn't convinced.

'Listen, Delroy,' said Bradman. 'Remember that time the police shoved you in their panda car? Remember 'ow up-tight you was 'bout it?'

'Yes,' said Delroy.

'What 'ad you done to deserve that?'

'Nothing.'

'Exactly. If they do that to you when you've done not'in', perhaps you should do somet'in' they should be annoyed 'bout, an' try an' get away wit' it. You're only gettin' you own back.'

Delroy puzzled over the logic of Bradman's argument. There did seem to be some sense in it.

'Come on,' said Bradman. 'Let's go to your yard. I want to 'ear these discs.'

Delroy forgot about his doubts. He wanted to hear the song as well. They ran across the pavement as a 52 bus pulled into the kerb and jumped on.

Five minutes later, Delroy was excitedly opening his front door. Bradman already had the record out of his bag. They were just hurrying up the stairs to Delroy's bedroom when Mr Ellis walked into the hall.

'Where are you going?' he demanded.

Delroy was home early for once. He hadn't expected his father to be in.

'We're going to play some records,' he said.

'You'd better come down here,' said Mr Ellis.

The two boys exchanged glances. Their smiles went. It looked as though they weren't going to hear their song after all.

Mr Ellis's face was cloudy. There was no sign of his usual ingratiating charm. The two boys stood nervously in front of him.

'Take your hat off in the house,' said Mr Ellis to Bradman. 'Haven't you got any manners?'

Bradman hastily pulled his tam off. His hair was revealed. It was tightly plaited close to the skull in long furrows. It was a style he adopted from time to time. It attracted Mr Ellis's attention.

'Look at your hair,' he exclaimed with disgust. 'I don't know what your parents are thinking of allowing you to do it like that. It's a disgrace.'

Bradman's eyes began to narrow with resentment. Delroy knew that his father disliked any kind of style that was different. He would have liked to have plaited his own hair, but there was no chance with his father around.

Mr Ellis was still concentrating on Bradman.

'You're a bad boy,' he said. 'Keep away from here. I don't want to see you in this house ever again.'

Bradman's eyes had narrowed still further. His mouth and chin were tense. But he didn't say anything.

'Go on,' said Mr Ellis. He jerked his head in the direction of the door.

60

Still without saying anything, Bradman turned and went out.

Delroy watched him go. He was angry at the way his father had spoken to his friend. He felt shame, too, that his father should have shown him up like this in front of Bradman. He didn't voice his feelings though. He knew his turn was coming.

'In here,' said Mr Ellis. 'I want to talk to you.'

They went into the front room. Delroy sat down and waited for the onslaught. It was an effort to subdue himself. He wanted to defy his father. He wanted to tell him what he thought of him. But he couldn't bring himself to do it. He knew he couldn't. He would just have to sit there and take what was coming to him.

'Let's get one thing straight,' his father began. 'That's the last time I go up to that school because of you.'

The hardness and bitterness in Mr Ellis's voice told Delroy that his father also had his pride. Going up to the school was a humiliation to him. He didn't like the headmaster having him in his office and telling him off. Because that was the way his father took it. Delroy was the person being reprimanded, but as far as his father was concerned, he was the one in the stand on trial.

'I mean it,' Mr Ellis went on. 'It's the last time. If you get into any more trouble, you'll have to find your own way out. I'm not going to help you.'

Delroy almost snorted with disbelief. When had his father ever been any help? That was the last thing Delroy would ask. He had managed so far without it. He would go on managing.

'There have got to be some changes,' continued Mr Ellis. 'For a start, that Bradman doesn't come round here again. And you don't go round to his place. In fact, you don't go out at night at all. You stay in and do your homework. I expect you to come home straight from school. No hanging around or seeing your friends. No more wasting your time on basketball. Because if you're not home straight from school, there'll be trouble. Is that clear?'

'Yes, Dad,' said Delroy.

He didn't see what else he could say. His words gave agreement, but the expression on his face showed something quite different.

'What was all that stuff about the headmaster writing a letter?' Mr Ellis asked suddenly as though he had just remembered it. His voice was full of suspicion.

'I don't know,' said Delroy, feigning innocence.

'You'd better not,' said Mr Ellis darkly. 'If I find out you've been stealing letters again, you'll wish you'd never been born.'

Delroy kept very still. He often did this when there was a crisis, as though by keeping absolutely immobile, the danger would go away. It didn't always work, but this time Delroy was lucky. His father didn't pursue the question of the letter.

'Right,' said Mr Ellis. 'You can begin now. Up to your room. Get on with your homework.'

Delroy stood up and went to his bedroom. Inside, he closed the door and leaned his back against it for a moment, his teeth grinding. He was furious. Who did his father think he was, ordering him about like that? He was old enough to have a life of his own, and here was his father laying down new rules, harsher rules, which Delroy knew would be impossible to keep. It was too much. He wanted to hit out. The ideal target was his father. Oh, how he would have loved to knock that self-righteous expression off his face. But he knew he didn't have the nerve. The mere fact that he had thought of it made him quake a little. Still, he had to vent his resentment on something. The nearest object was the bed. He kicked it really hard.

Then he sat down on the edge, his head in his hands, and stared at the floor. Gradually, his resentment faded and gloom took over. His father's words sank in. Straight home from school. No more basketball. No going out at night. No more friends. It was all too much. He didn't think he would be able to endure it all.

And there was still the business of the letter. He had a feeling he hadn't heard the last of that yet.

FOURTEEN

In spite of his sense of grievance after his father's warning, Delroy renewed his efforts to stay out of trouble at school. It was a strain to start with. Whenever a friend began chatting to him in class or joking, Delroy found himself automatically responding. It took a real struggle of will-power to pull himself away when he saw the teacher's eye moving in his direction and get back to work.

He managed to avoid notice for a whole morning. He began to feel more optimistic. Perhaps it wasn't going to be too difficult after all. It was only at the end of the last period before lunch that danger threatened. He was held behind after the other pupils had gone. Mr Kemp wanted to know where his homework was.

'I forgot to bring it,' said Delroy, blurting out the first idea that came into his mind.

'That's an old one,' said Mr Kemp.

'It's true, sir, it's true,' protested Delroy, excitedly, a bright grin all over his face. He tried to give the impression that he knew some pupils used this excuse but that his excuse was in fact real. He was an eager, hard-working pupil who would never tell a lie.

'Are you sure?' asked Mr Kemp, his certainty weakened by this display.

'Of course I am,' said Delroy earnestly. 'I'll bring it tomorrow.'

'You had better do so,' warned Mr Kemp, letting him off.

'Yes, yes, I will,' promised Delroy, as he hurried out of the room.

He sighed with relief. That was a close one.

He was now late for lunch. If he didn't get down quickly, he'd have to wait hours in the queue. As he entered the foyer, he realized he was already too late. The line of hungry boys spread the full length of the entrance hall. Mr Frobisher was on duty, yelling at boys to keep in

63

single file. If they so much as stepped forward to talk to the boy in front of them, Mr Frobisher would manhandle them back into place.

Delroy went and sat on one of the seats alongside the window. If he were clever, he might be able to get into the queue and join his friends when Mr Frobisher's back was turned. He watched vigilantly, waiting for the right moment. There was some disturbance inside the dining room, and one of the lunch supervisors called Mr Frobisher to sort things out. This was Delroy's chance. He dived into the line beside Bradman, ten boys from the top of the queue. Bradman welcomed him, and then they both tried to look as unobtrusive as possible.

When Mr Frobisher returned to the foyer, he walked down the line, making sure the boys were in single file. He went past Delroy. Delroy breathed a silent delighted sigh of relief for Bradman's benefit. Then he felt a hand on his arm. Mr Frobisher had come back.

'What are you doing here, Ellis?' the teacher demanded. 'You weren't in the queue before.'

'Yes, I was,' protested Delroy.

'You've pushed in,' said Mr Frobisher.

'No, I haven't,' said Delroy, getting angry and pulling his arm away from Mr Frobisher's grasp.

'He was here all the time,' said Bradman, coming to the aid of his friend.

But Mr Frobisher was having none of it.

'Get to the back of the queue,' he said.

'He was here all the time,' repeated Bradman.

'If you've got any sense,' said Mr Frobisher, turning to Bradman, 'you won't get involved in this. I'm not an idiot. I know perfectly well who was in the queue and who wasn't. And Ellis pushed in.'

'I didn't,' protested Delroy again. His face had clouded over angrily. He was glaring defiantly at Mr Frobisher.

'Are you going to do what you are told?' demanded Mr Frobisher, laying down an ultimatum.

The results of recent encounters with Mr Frobisher and the realization of the need to keep out of trouble rushed through Delroy's mind. He shrugged himself free of the queue and stamped off, muttering angry thoughts about Mr Frobisher on the way.

'What did you say, boy?' roared Mr Frobisher's voice after him.

Delroy stopped in his tracks.

'I didn't say anything,' he mumbled.

'Come here when I'm talking to you.'

Delroy froze, deliberating in his mind whether or not to obey. He turned slowly and approached Mr Frobisher.

'What did you say?' again demanded the teacher.

'I didn't say anything,' said Delroy sulkily.

'You'd better watch your step, my lad,' said Mr Frobisher threateningly, 'or else you're going to be in serious trouble. Now get to the back of the queue.'

Delroy walked slowly to the end of the line. He kept his mouth under control this time, but his eyes were talking murder.

'Frobisher's really got it in for you,' said Bradman when Delroy eventually joined his friend at the table with his dinner.

'He's out to get you,' said Ant'ny.

'You'll have to watch you step,' warned Bradman.

'Why should 'e?' asked Ant'ny. 'The way these teachers throw their weight 'bout. Who they t'ink they are?'

'Did you 'ear 'bout Leroy?' asked Paul excitedly. ''E was suspended this mornin'.'

'Oh no,' exclaimed Ant'ny. 'What was that for?'

''E was askin' another boy for some money,' said Paul.

'Oh no,' repeated Ant'ny. 'That's not fair.'

Mr Frobisher walked past the table, keeping an eye on the behaviour of the boys. Delroy and his friends looked at him with accusing eyes until he was past. Then they went on with their dinner.

Before long, Mr Frobisher was back. He pointed to a dirty plate that had been left on the table.

'Who left that?' he demanded.

There was a long pause before Bradman finally said, 'I don' know. Whoever was 'ere before me, I suppose.'

'Take it back with your own plates when you've finished, Ellis,' said Mr Frobisher.

Delroy seethed. Why did he have to take the plate back, he asked himself. He hadn't left it there. It wasn't his job to take back dirty plates. Then Delroy remembered his previous row with Mr Frobisher over picking up paper from the floor, and he said nothing.

He was conscious as he went on with his dinner of Mr Frobisher's eyes constantly turning in his direction to make sure that he hadn't left without taking the extra plate back.

When he rose after finishing his meal, Mr Frobisher walked towards his table. Their eyes met for a moment. Then Delroy lowered his. He put the dirty plate on top of his own and took it to the hatch in the kitchen.

''As anyone got a fag?' asked Bradman as they walked into the foyer. 'I'm dyin' for a drag.'

'I've got one,' said Paul. 'But I've only got one.'

'That's all right,' said Bradman. 'We can share it.'

The safest place in the school for a quick smoke was the boys' toilets. One or other of their friends was always hanging about outside near the light switch. If a teacher approached, he would turn the light switch on and off as a warning.

They hurried to the toilet. Paul took a crumpled cigarette packet out of his pocket and extracted the last remaining cigarette. He lit it and pulled deeply on it. The smoke he exhaled hung like a wreath in the cold, still air.

'That's better,' breathed Paul with satisfaction.

'Come on,' said Bradman. 'It's my turn.'

Paul passed the cigarette to him, and Bradman took a long draw.

'I needed that,' said Bradman.

Since Ant'ny didn't smoke, the cigarette went next to Delroy.

'Did you see the match on Saturday?' asked Paul.

'I don' know why you support Arsenal,' said Ant'ny. 'They're a load of wankers.'

'They're a good team,' protested Paul.

'They don' know if they're comin' or goin',' said Ant'ny.

The cigarette had reached Bradman again, and he puffed on it gratefully.

Then they were suddenly aware of a shadow in the doorway. Two things happened simultaneously. Mr Frobisher came round the corner, and Bradman instinctively threw the cigarette into the urinal. The first thought that went through Delroy's mind was, oh, God, I've been caught again. The second was, where were those bloody guards? Why hadn't they given them warning?

'Right, all of you,' said Mr Frobisher, 'school detention for smoking.'

'But I don' smoke,' protested Ant'ny.

'Did you see me? Did you see me?' protested Delroy.

Paul and Bradman kept quiet.

'I don't need to see you,' said Mr Frobisher. 'The fact that you are here is enough.'

'That's not fair,' said Ant'ny.

'What's fairness got to do with it?' asked Mr Frobisher. 'We're fed up with you doing what you're not supposed to do. So if you're here when someone's smoking, you've got nobody to blame but yourself.'

'Did you see me? Did you see me?' repeated Delroy, getting more and more excited.

'Don't you use that tone with me,' warned Mr Frobisher, 'or you'll be in worse trouble.'

'I think we ought to see the headmaster,' said Ant'ny. 'It's not fair. I don' even smoke.'

'See who you like,' said Mr Frobisher. 'But as far as I'm concerned, you've all got a school detention for smoking.'

He turned on his heel and stalked off.

'Come on,' said Ant'ny. 'Let's go an' see Johnson.'

'What good will that do?' asked Paul.

'You never know,' said Ant'ny. 'It sometimes works.'

'But we were smokin',' said Paul.

'What's that got to do wit' it?' asked Bradman. 'He didn' actually catch us, did he?'

When they reached the headmaster's office, they were just in time to meet Mr Frobisher coming out.

'I beat you to it, didn't I?' he said maliciously.

The boys looked at each other and didn't know what to say.

'Come on,' said Ant'ny at last. 'We might at least try.'

They knocked at the door.

'Come in,' called Mr Johnson.

They entered and ranged themselves sheepishly before the headmaster.

Mr Johnson looked up from what he was writing. 'What's the problem?' he asked.

There was an embarrassed silence, before Bradman pushed himself forward as spokesman. 'Is it fair,' he asked, 'for somebody to get a school detention for smokin' when 'e wasn't smokin'?'

'But you were smoking,' said Mr Johnson. 'Mr Frobisher caught you with a cigarette in your hand.'

Bradman considered this for a moment, and then magnanimously admitted, 'All right, so I did 'ave a cigarette in my 'and, but was I smokin'? Mr Frobisher didn' see me smokin'.'

Mr Johnson tried to be patient.

'You're splitting hairs, Bradman. I can't imagine what other reason you would have for holding a cigarette in your hand if not to smoke it.'

'All right,' said Bradman. 'I 'ad a cigarette in my 'and. I admit that. An' I might 'ave been goin' to smoke it. But that doesn't prove anyt'in'. The others didn't 'ave cigarettes. Ant'ny don' even smoke.'

Mr Johnson breathed out wearily.

'You've been told this before, Bradman, time and time again. You know perfectly well that people smoke in the boys' toilets, and if someone is there, he is likely to get the blame as much as anyone else caught with a cigarette in his hand.'

'But I don' smoke,' said Ant'ny.

'Hard luck,' said Mr Johnson, getting annoyed. 'If you don't want to be classed with the others, you should keep away.'

'I'm not doin' the detention,' said Ant'ny.

'That's your look-out,' said Mr Johnson. 'You know what will happen if you don't do your detention.'

'It's not fair,' said Delroy.

'Life's not fair,' said Mr Johnson. 'And it's about time

you realized that fact and adjusted your behaviour accordingly. Think about all the times you've done something wrong and you haven't been caught. Is that fair? I don't notice you coming to my office and complaining that you've done something wrong and haven't been punished for it.'

'That's different,' said Bradman.

'Yes,' said Mr Johnson ironically, 'of course it is. You want everything loaded in your favour, don't you?'

The headmaster stared at the boys for a moment while they considered the situation.

'Look,' he said, 'as far as I am concerned, Mr Frobisher found one of you with a cigarette. The air was full of cigarette smoke. There were three other boys there. And you are equally guilty. If it happens that on this occasion you are innocent, then take into account all the other times you have been smoking and haven't been caught.'

'I'm not doin' a school detention,' repeated Ant'ny.

'You had better,' warned Mr Johnson, 'or else you will be in worse trouble.'

The interview was clearly at an end. There was no point in discussing the matter further. The boys trooped out of the office.

'It's just like the 'ead to take a teacher's word for it 'gainst ours,' said Bradman.

'That's the last time I go to 'im', said Paul.

'I think 'e's scared of old Frobisher,' said Bradman.

'I'm not doin' the detention,' went on Ant'ny.

'Oh, shut you mout',' said Paul sullenly.

Ant'ny seemed surprised at this sudden aggression on the part of Paul. He looked at Delroy.

'Are you doin' it?' he asked.

'I'll think about it,' replied Delroy.

He couldn't afford to get into more trouble. Perhaps it would be better simply to do the detention and get it over with. At least that way his father would probably never get to hear about it. But it still didn't seem fair. Mr Frobisher hadn't actually caught him with a cigarette in his mouth or in his hand.

It was all Mr Frobisher's fault. Delroy had been getting on fine in his new role as the well-behaved pupil. And then Mr Frobisher had come along and spoiled it all. Everything would be all right if only there weren't people like Mr Frobisher about. Delroy began to think that Bradman had been right when he had said that Mr Frobisher had got it in for him.

FIFTEEN

But the incident wasn't finished with yet. Mrs Lasky wanted to see Delroy after registration.

'I hear you've been caught smoking,' she said.

Immediately Delroy sprang to the defensive.

'I wasn't smoking,' he protested. 'Mr Frobisher didn't see me smoking.'

'Oh, come off it, Delroy,' said Mrs Lasky in exasperation. 'We haven't time for these games.'

Delroy subsided and began to sulk.

'Delroy,' said Mrs Lasky, more in sorrow than in anger, 'what are we going to do with you?'

Delroy looked up. He was uncertain how to respond.

'Your parents were up only yesterday,' continued Mrs Lasky, 'and you said you would try to behave. Then this happens.'

'I am trying,' said Delroy, playing for sympathy.

'You're not trying hard enough,' said Mrs Lasky.

Delroy could sense his form teacher watching him and studying him. She seemed to be appraising him, weighing up how much of his attitude was genuine and how much was an act put on to ingratiate himself with her. He kept his eyes down. Mrs Lasky was no fool.

'I know being caught smoking isn't a serious crime,' said Mrs Lasky. 'But you shouldn't be getting into this kind of trouble. You're a bright boy, and you ought to be concentrating on your work and getting the results you deserve.'

Delroy didn't say anything.

'I sometimes wonder,' went on Mrs Lasky, 'whether

you believe us when we tell you you're bright. Do you?'

'No,' said Delroy.

'Don't you think you're bright?'

'No.'

It was an automatic response. Delroy just didn't know. At times he felt he was brighter than the others. And then again, he wasn't sure. How could he tell?

'But Delroy, listen,' said Mrs Lasky. 'I've had a lot of experience teaching pupils and seeing them grow up. Much of my time is spent in working out how bright or how able pupils are. So if I say you are bright it's not just some guess I've pulled out of the air. It's based on a few years of knowing young people and teaching them and studying them. And it's not just me. Other teachers say the same. Don't you believe us?'

'I'm not sure,' said Delroy.

Mrs Lasky looked depressed.

'Then I don't know how to convince you.'

She looked away, her forehead lined with thought. Delroy stole a quick glance at her. He really did like Mrs Lasky. He felt ashamed at causing her all this worry. She did try to help him, he was certain.

Mrs Lasky returned to the attack.

'Don't you think it's worth working hard so you can get a decent job?'

'What's the point?' asked Delroy.

'What d'you mean?'

'There aren't any jobs for people like me.'

'I don't understand you.'

Mrs Lasky sounded genuinely baffled.

'Even if I tried hard,' said Delroy bitterly, 'I wouldn't get a decent job. All the decent jobs go to white people.'

Mrs Lasky looked appalled.

'That's nonsense,' she exploded. 'I know things are hard, but I can give you the names of any number of black boys from this school who have gone on to good jobs — because they've worked at it and deserved it.'

Delroy didn't believe her.

'All right,' went on Mrs Lasky. 'There are cases of prejudice and discrimination. But they're getting fewer

71

and fewer, and anyway, that's no reason for not trying.'

Still Delroy didn't believe her.

'What about the police then?' he asked. 'They're prejudiced, aren't they? They're all National Front.'

'That's just not true,' protested Mrs Lasky.

'Yes, they are.'

'There are bound to be one or two prejudiced individuals in any group of people,' conceded Mrs Lasky, 'but that doesn't mean they're all racists. What about Sergeant East?' She was referring to the policeman from the Juvenile Bureau who came in sometimes to talk to the social studies class. 'I've sat in on some of his lessons, and he strikes me as being very fair and honest. You can ask him anything, and he'll give you a straight answer. He's all right, isn't he?'

'I suppose so,' said Delroy reluctantly.

'I think you've just not met the right kind of policeman,' said Mrs Lasky.

Delroy knew she meant this as a joke, but he didn't find it very funny.

His form teacher became serious again.

'You needn't think you hold a monopoly of discrimination,' she said.

'What d'you mean?' asked Delroy.

'Look at me. What am I?'

Delroy was surprised at the question. He didn't really know what she was getting at.

'For a start,' she explained. 'I'm a woman, and there are some employers who don't like women working for them. And for a second thing, I'm Jewish. Does that mean anything to you?'

'Not really,' said Delroy.

'When I was your age, I had to put up with people saying things, calling me names. It was unpleasant. Many's the time I ran home from school and cried because of something hurtful one of my classmates had said. But I didn't let that stop me. In fact, I think it spurred me on. I was determined that I would damn well show them. And I did. I don't think I've done too badly. Do you see the point I'm making?'

'I don't know,' said Delroy evasively.

72

'Oh yes you do,' said Mrs Lasky. 'It doesn't matter whether you're black or Jewish in a prejudiced world. What matters is what you've got inside you. If you've got enough determination, you can stand up against anyone. And what you've got to do, Delroy, is to kick the white world in the teeth – not literally, not by being violent, but by developing what you've got inside you. By showing them that you're as good as they are — perhaps even better. You have the ability. Why don't you do it?'

Delroy didn't know. It all seemed so difficult. It was all very well for Mrs Lasky to talk: she had done it in her way, and it was over with. But for Delroy, it hadn't even begun yet.

Why did teachers have to go on at him like this? When they did, the only defence was to go into a kind of coma, to abstract himself from the situation, and let the words flow over his head.

'Anyway,' said Mrs Lasky, coming back to the present, 'you know you've got a detention for smoking.'

'Yes.'

'Right then. You'd better do it tomorrow night.'

Delroy was suddenly awake again.

'But I've got a basketball match tomorrow night,' he said.

It would be too much to have to miss that because of Mr Frobisher. The fact that his father had told him he wasn't to play basketball any more was conveniently forgotten.

'You should have thought of that before,' said Mrs Lasky.

'But it's important,' said Delroy becoming agitated. 'It's the cup against Northlands.'

Mrs Lasky softened.

'All right,' she said. 'I'll make an allowance this once. You can do your detention next week.'

'Thanks, miss,' said Delroy.

He sensed that the interview was coming to an end.

'And make sure you play well tomorrow night.'

'I will, miss,' said Delroy, and he flashed his form teacher one of his special smiles.

73

'And remember. We can't go on making allowances for you.'

Delroy was free to go. He raced down the stairs and out of school. If he was quick, Bradman, Ant'ny and Paul might still be waiting for him at the gate. It was just like Mrs Lasky to keep him back. Then he remembered his father's warning that he was to go straight home and that he wasn't to see Bradman again. His pace slowed. Perhaps he had better just catch the bus and not go with his friends to the shopping centre as usual.

He thought about what Mrs Lasky had said. Was she really worried about what happened to him? For a moment he believed that possibly she was. But then he dismissed the idea from his mind. How could she be? She was just a teacher like all the others.

Bradman, Ant'ny and Paul were still at the main gate when Delroy arrived. Before he could make his excuses and go home alone, Bradman asked, 'You comin' to the disco tonight?'

'What disco?' Delroy asked.

'At the Paradise. Franklyn's doin' the sound. 'E's super. 'E's my cousin.'

Bradman seemed to have uncles and cousins everywhere. As far as Delroy could make out, half the school was related to him.

'I don't know,' said Delroy.

'Come on,' coaxed Bradman. 'It'll be a great night.'

'I'll have to see,' said Delroy, playing for time.

He really didn't know how he would be able to make it, the position he was in, though he was sorely tempted. One false move, and his father would be down on him like a ton of bricks.

'I've got to go straight home now,' he said.

'Be like that,' mocked Bradman.

''E's gettin' as bad as Stephen,' said Paul.

'Yeah,' agreed Ant'ny. 'Next t'ing you know 'e'll be doin' 'is 'omework.'

'Shut you mout',' snapped Delroy.

'Who's gwone make me?' challenged Ant'ny.

'I am,' said Delroy.

74

'You an' whose army?' asked Ant'ny.

He and Delroy squared up to each other, their fists clenched and their faces angrily brooding.

'Aw, come off it, you two,' said Bradman, coming between them. He turned to Delroy. 'You'll be there tonight then. Call for me.'

'I'll see,' said Delroy, and he hurried off before any of the others could add their persuasion, and before his resolution to try to obey his father faltered.

SIXTEEN

After supper that evening, Delroy sat watching the television. He wasn't really looking at the programme. In fact, he couldn't have said what the programme was. His mind was far away. He was thinking about the disco and wondering whether he dared go. He wanted to go. The only thing that prevented him was his father. There was that ultimatum that he wasn't to go out at night. His father had meant it.

But it was boring here, just sitting watching television. Barry was glued to the table, doing his homework. His mother was in the kitchen, washing up.

Bradman was fun to be with. He was free to do what he liked. When Delroy was with Bradman there was no one to order him about or tell him off. They always had a good time.

The strain of the day was beginning to have its effect as well. Delroy had made such an effort to behave himself and, on the whole, he had succeeded. If it hadn't been for Mr Frobisher, the day could have been called perfect. He had paid attention in class. He had got on with his work. He had kept away from his friends after school. Now he felt that he deserved a reward.

He remembered that his father had told his mother that morning at breakfast that he would be working late. He was a salesman. Delroy wasn't sure what he actually sold, but he had to travel around the area, making deals.

Some of his calls had to be in the evening — at least that's what he told his wife.

An idea began to form in Delroy's mind. If his father wasn't going to be home until late, then there was a chance. He could slip out to the disco and be back before his father was home. He had done it before and got away with it. No one would know. It was too good an opportunity to miss.

Delroy jumped up from his seat so abruptly that Barry's hand slipped and his pencil accidentally made an extra line on the diagram he was drawing.

'Blast, man,' he said.

But Delroy had already left the room.

He put his head round the door of the kitchen.

'I'm going upstairs to do my homework,' he said, 'and then I'm going to bed.'

'All right,' said his mother without looking up from the sink.

In his bedroom, Delroy put the light on and spread some of his school books over the table by the bed. If somebody did come up while he was out, he could say he had gone for a walk. But nobody would come up.

Delroy pulled on a thick sweater and on top of that a corduroy jerkin. He opened the door and listened carefully. The drone of the television and the clink of crockery came to him from below. Still, he hesitated. Should he leave the light on? If his mother saw the light under the door, she would assume that he was there and working. On the other hand, she might go in. It would be safer to switch the light off. Then if his mother noticed, she would think he had just gone to bed.

He closed the door of his darkened bedroom behind him, and started to creep down the stairs. He remembered to avoid the second step from the top. He reached the front door safely and eased it open. Then he was outside. He pushed the Yale lock back cautiously so that it slipped into position slowly and silently as he pulled the door shut.

The garden gate was the next obstacle. He lifted the latch and squeezed through, quietly closing the gate behind him. Then he was off, running down the street, his

76

trainers making no noise on the pavement. He leaped in the air. He opened his mouth and a shriek of joy almost escaped from him, but he remembered in time and swallowed the bubble of delight that was rising within him.

As he reached the bottom of the street, a bus was cruising along the main road. He raced towards it. The bus had come to a halt at the bus stop, and Delroy was just in time to jump on as it set off again.

Bradman was expecting him. As usual, the flat was full of people.

"Ello, there,' said Errol. 'Where you off to then, man? Out wit' one o' you chicks?' He laughed mockingly.

Delroy was delighted to be noticed. Through the smoky atmosphere behind Errol, he could see that they had already begun their game of cards. Faces turned to look at him curiously.

'You look after little Bradman,' said Errol. 'You know 'e goin' to get into whole 'eap o' trouble one o' these days.'

Errol staggered a few steps and held on to the door-post for support. He must have been at the rum bottle already, Delroy thought.

'Shut you mout',' snapped Bradman.

Errol leaned his head back, and a great roar of laughter burst from his barrel-like chest. He put his hands on his hips and started flapping his elbows, at the same time making clucking noises.

"Urry up, little Bradman,' he said, 'or all the little chicks will 'ave flew.'

'Come on,' said Bradman, ignoring his brother's teasing.

They felt their way down the stairs from the flat. When they reached ground level, they were off, running through the streets, their one aim in life to arrive at the Paradise as quickly as possible.

They could hear the noise of the sound system belting out of the youth club long before they reached it. The beat pulsed vibrantly in the night air. Delroy's body began to tingle with excitement.

Bradman paid admission for them both and then they

77

were inside. The Paradise had been transformed for the occasion. It was a dark, mysterious world. Coloured lights momentarily lit up and then flashed off again. The insistent bass of the music was so strong that the whole building throbbed with it. There was already a fair number of people there. No one was actually dancing, but along the walls and in the corners, bodies were bobbing up and down to the rhythm, heads nodding backwards and forwards, hips swaying, knees bending.

At the far end of the hall which had been cleared of billiard tables and table-tennis tables was the sound system. Bradman made straight for it.

'Hi, Franklyn,' he said.

'Hi, boy,' said Franklyn.

Bradman's cousin was very big and very black. His hair was arranged in the most magnificent set of dreadlocks Delroy had ever seen. Waxed and tightly plaited, they hung out all around his head. He was wearing jeans and a singlet on which was emblazoned a black face. Around his neck was a scarf in Rasta colours — green, gold and scarlet. His fingers were adorned with rings, and there were gold bangles on his wrist. Delroy was envious of Bradman for having a cousin like this.

'It gwone be a good night tonight, eh?' said Franklyn.

'You bet,' said Bradman.

They had to shout to make themselves heard above the sound of the music. All around Franklyn was spread the sound equipment. Delroy gazed at it with awe.

'Hey, man,' Franklyn said to Bradman. 'You can do I a big favour when this gig over. You can 'elp I pack up this stuff.'

'Sure t'ing, man,' said Bradman.

'Then you come back to my yard, eh? Carry on the celebration.'

'Sure t'ing, man,' said Bradman again.

Delroy hoped that Franklyn would ask him as well, but the sounds man was too busy sorting out his records even to notice Delroy. He would have given anything to be involved in just a tiny part of the glamour of it all. He breathed in the whole atmosphere so that his chest swelled

78

to bursting point with it. This was better than being at home, stuck in the house over his books. Here there were people. Here there was excitement, noise, music and movement. Here there was life.

By now, more people had arrived. The hall had begun to fill up. There were even people in the middle of the floor, mainly girls, writhing and moving to the beat of the music.

When the record came to an end, Franklyn spoke into the microphone.

'I and I is gwone 'ave a big time tonight. For why? 'Cos I and I is 'scapin' from tribulation. Yeah, man!'

There was a cheer from the audience, and the next record burst out into the hall. The pounding rhythm established itself before the high-pitched voices of the group came in with the words:
'Africa – a – a,
Africa, the Zion land, oh
That the place I long to be, oh
That the place I long to be . . . .'
'Great song,' said Bradman, yelling in Delroy's ear.
'Yeah, I know,' said Delroy. 'I've got it.'
'You 'ave? Can I loan it some time?'
'Sure, man, sure.'

More people joined the dancers on the floor. The movements became wilder and more daring. Dancers experimented with new steps and leaps and twists.

In a corner, Delroy found Ant'ny, Paul and the others. He admired the way they were sharply dressed, their tightly-fitted shiny waistcoats, their Cecil Gee trousers and their pointed shoes. His father wouldn't let him buy clothes like that. Their faces were shining and excited.

'Oh no, man,' cried Ant'ny when he saw Delroy. 'Look who 'ere!'

'Hi, Delroy,' greeted Paul. 'I thought you wasn't comin'.'

'Well, I changed my mind,' said Delroy.

'That's your privilege,' said Paul.

'You girl, you,' mocked Ant'ny.

He roared with appreciation at his own joke and

flicked his fingers in the air.

Delroy didn't take offence. He knew it was just Ant'ny's way of having fun.

The laugh suddenly vanished from Ant'ny's face. His features became stern and clouded over. He was staring at two white girls who were dancing together.

'What they let 'em in for?' he demanded resentfully.

'You know you fancy 'em,' said Paul teasingly.

'Get out,' said Ant'ny angrily. 'I don' like pork.'

He continued to glare disapprovingly at the girls as they shuffled past.

Another record had begun. The words boomed out over the speakers:

'Babylon is lookin' down 'pon I,

Is lookin' down 'pon I . . . .'

The boys started to sway to the rhythm.

'Ain't that Eddie's sister?' asked Paul, drawing their attention to a group of black girls standing against the wall near them.

They all turned to look. The girls were bunched together, faces expressionless, bodies wriggling to the beat of the music.

'Which one?' said Paul.

'The big one,' said Paul.

'Yes,' said Delroy. 'That's Shirley.'

Ant'ny focused his eyes on Shirley and coolly examined her.

'I bet you fancy 'er,' said Paul.

'No, I don',' said Ant'ny. 'She too big.'

'You know you wants to make banana bread wit' she,' jeered Paul, putting on his Jamaican voice.

Ant'ny burned Paul up with his famous glare of contempt. But his eyes returned to Shirley to have another inspection.

Noticing the boys' attention, the girls began to whisper among themselves, and started giggling. Shirley gave the boys a brazen stare as if to say, who d'you think you're looking at. It wouldn't have surprised Delroy if she had stuck her tongue out at them.

'Aw, this is grim,' said Ant'ny.

And he suddenly leaped out on to the floor like a swimmer jumping into the deep end of the pool. Delroy and the others found themselves drawn in too. They formed an undulating mass. Heads jerked backwards and forwards or from side to side. Their bodies became separated at the waists, the top halfs and the bottom halfs in their movements seeming to have no relation to each other. Arms and legs soared double-jointed into the air. They strutted like turkey-cocks and threw Kung Fu kicks that narrowly missed each other's heads. They jumped up, twisted round and landed facing the opposite direction. They moved in on each other, menacingly close, only just avoiding collision, and then burst away in a frenzy of loose-limbed activity.

Delroy and his friends pretended to be totally self-absorbed, but every now and then a quick flick of the eye-lash showed that they were concerned about how the girls were taking their performance. As for the girls, they tried to ignore the boys, but they couldn't prevent their eyes from veering round to gaze mesmerized by their contortions. It took a real effort of will for them to drag their eyes away.

At the end of the dance Delroy was hot. His face was gleaming with sweat. He was wearing too many clothes. He felt the need for something to drink. He had enough money to buy himself a Coke. It meant that he would have to walk home, but that didn't matter. He had forgotten about home. Now the thought of it came rushing back to him. Would his mother have discovered that he had gone out? He was suddenly cold and shivery under his sweat. Then he shrugged the thought away. What did he care? He was having a good time. This was life. If his parents didn't like it, then that was just too bad.

He went to the counter and bought himself a Coke. A girl passed him and gave him a wide-eyed stare. It was only when she had gone that he realized it was Shirley. An immense sense of elation arose within him. He suddenly felt full of himself. Perhaps she fancied him. The idea that girls might be interested in him had never really occurred to Delroy before.

81

He went back to Ant'ny and the others in their corner feeling very confident and superior. Paul was talking to one of the girls, but the two groups still kept their separate identities. Paul began to dance with the girls. Delroy and his other friends let out jeers and cat-calls. Paul was concentrating so much on his elaborate foot and arm work that he didn't seem to notice.

Bradman reappeared. Delroy could smell the sweet smell of ganja clinging to his clothing. Bradman had been out the back for a quick drag at the weed. It was not Delroy's scene, but what Bradman did was his business.

'Ain't Franklyn great?' exclaimed Bradman, his eyes shining bright with appreciation.

'Yeah, crazy,' agreed Delroy.

'A great gig,' said Bradman.

He was about to add something else when there was a scream at the bottom of the hall near the sound system. It rose shrill and cutting above the noise of the music. Then it was swallowed up in angry shouts.

A surge of people swept towards the spot. Delroy was pushed forward with it. Everyone wanted to find out what had happened. There were arms and elbows and bodies everywhere, struggling and fighting to reach the scene of the disturbance.

Over the heads of the people in front of him, Delroy could see a girl. She was screaming and crying and wailing. She was holding on to a boy slumped against her shoulder. Suddenly the fluorescent lights were switched on. Delroy blinked at the unnatural brightness of them. A white youth worker pushed his way through the crowd.

'Now what's happened?' he yelled.

He took hold of the boy and lifted his head up to the light. Delroy could see the bright red of the blood against the brown skin of the boy's face. The wound looked clean-cut as though caused by a razor or a sharp knife. The assailant was nowhere to be seen. He had already made his escape. The girl went on sobbing.

More youth workers appeared. They began to usher the dancers out. There were squeals and shouts of protest, but they didn't do any good. The youth workers moved steadily forward clearing the hall. The wounded boy and the girl had disappeared. They had been taken into another room. It was all over as quickly as it had started.

Delroy and Bradman managed to evade the cordon formed by the youth workers. They made for Franklyn who was already getting on with the job of packing up.

'What was all that, guy?' Bradman asked excitedly.

''E probably pinch someone else girlfriend,' said Franklyn unconcerned. 'It 'appen all the time.'

Franklyn was stacking the records away.

'You gwone 'elp me, boy?' he asked.

'Yeah, man,' said Bradman.

Suddenly, Delroy felt left out. Already Bradman was busy disconnecting plugs from the switch-board. He and Franklyn seemed to have forgotten he was still there.

'See you,' said Delroy.

'Yeah, man,' said Bradman without looking up.

Outside, it was cold and dark. There were still a few people hanging around. Paul was there talking to a girl. He had his arm around her waist. Delroy couldn't be certain, but it might have been Shirley. There was no one else there that he knew. Ant'ny and his other friends had disappeared. The evening was over. It was time for him to get back home.

All the way he worried about whether his mother had discovered that he had gone out and whether his father was back yet. If they knew about his outing, there would be all hell to pay. Delroy's silent footsteps on the pavement grew faster at the very thought of it.

As he turned into his street, he was reassured to see that his father's car was not parked outside the house. It could only be about ten o'clock. It was a good job the disco had finished early.

Delroy pushed open the garden gate. He noticed that the light was on in the front room. That didn't mean anything. With the sound of the television bubbling away, it would be easy to get up the stairs without being heard.

Inside his bedroom, nothing seemed to have been disturbed. His books were as he had left them. Delroy could relax. He grinned at his own cleverness. It hadn't been too difficult. He had been able to have a night out and see his friends in spite of his father. He would be able to do it again.

He gathered up his books and put them away. He wouldn't need them again that night.

SEVENTEEN

The sound of loud voices abruptly roused Delroy from sleep into consciousness. He felt confused, not knowing what time it was. Before he was fully awake, the door of his bedroom burst open, and the light was switched on.

Blinking his eyes, Delroy turned to look over his shoulder. His father was standing in the doorway. Through his screwed-up eyes, Delroy could see that he was breathing heavily and that he was very angry.

'What did I tell you about going out?' Mr Ellis demanded. 'Why don't you do what you're told?'

Mr Ellis strode over to the bed and tore the bedclothes off. Delroy half sat up, blinded still by the brightness of the light.

'Haven't I told you?' he roared. 'Haven't I?'

Then the flat of his father's hand struck Delroy so hard on the cheek that his head was knocked sideways and tears were jerked from his eyes.

'If you don't do what you're told,' continued Mr Ellis, 'then I'll disown you. I'll throw you out on the street.'

Each word Mr Ellis spoke was emphasized by a blow, a punch, or a slap on any part of Delroy's body that he could reach. Delroy drew himself up into a ball and tried to shield his face with his arms. He twisted this way and that to avoid the blows –– but contact was made. A stinging heat spread through his body.

'I'll throw you out on the street,' Mr Ellis repeated. 'Do you understand that? You can go and live somewhere else. I don't want you. Answer me then. Do you understand?'

'Yes, Dad,' mumbled Delroy from behind his arms.

'And another thing.' Delroy felt a sudden slap on his legs. 'That letter. I know you stole it. You must think I'm a fool.'

Delroy's arms were pulled away from his face and held in his father's crushing grip. There was no escape. Delroy was forced to look into his father's face, at his curling lip and blazing eyes.

'You listen carefully.' His father's voice was cold and ominous. 'You had better do what you are told in future. You come straight home from school and you stay here. If you don't, the front door will be bolted, and you can find somewhere else to live. Do you understand?'

'Yes, Dad.'

'That's my last word.'

Mr Ellis threw Delroy's arms back in his face and turned away. The light was switched off. The bedroom door was shut with a bang.

In the darkness, Delroy let the tenseness slip away. His body sank back into the mattress. He felt with his hands for the bedclothes and pulled them over him. It was then that the tears began to flow. They poured over the rims of his eyes and down his cheeks. All the features of his face were compressed hard against each other to prevent himself from sobbing and making a noise. He was not going to give his father the satisfaction of hearing him cry. But the tears could not be stopped.

'I hate him.' Delroy ground the words out. 'I hate him.'

And then there was his mother. She must have discovered that he had gone out. She must have told his father. She must have told him about the letter as well. She had let him down.

Delroy wiped the tears away with the backs of his hands, but they were to be replaced many times before he finally fell asleep.

EIGHTEEN

The memory of the beating his father had given him was still strong in Delroy's mind next morning. He could still feel the force of his father's open palm against his legs and arms. He still felt his body tingling with the heat and pain. His father's threats and demands still rang in his ears. And Delroy's resentment against his father burned as strong.

Never again would his father beat him, Delroy vowed. If he tried it, then Delroy would hit back. He didn't care if his father was bigger and more powerful than he was. He was a man now. He would stand up for himself. He wouldn't allow his father to touch him again. He wasn't a child any more who could be slapped and kept in his place.

But would he ever do it? Would he ever stand up to his father? Behind his brooding anger, doubt throbbed like an aching tooth. He was sure that an opportunity for defiance wouldn't be very long in coming. His father had laid down so many rules that Delroy just couldn't see himself keeping them all. He felt as though he was in a minefield. A single step in any direction could set off an explosion. And when that happened, would he be brave enough to face his father? He wasn't confident that he would be.

The first test was the cup match against Northlands. His father had said he wasn't to play basketball. He was to come straight home from school. If he played in the game he would be home late. His father had said that the front door would be bolted. He wouldn't let him in. Delroy knew his father wasn't joking. He didn't make jokes like that. He meant what he said, just as Delroy knew that his father would be quite ready to beat him again if he disobeyed him.

The question Delroy had to decide was whether or not to play in the basketball match. Throughout the day, it rolled round and round in his mind. With the monotony of a washing machine with its load of dirty linen, the problem whirled round without solution.

Even his friends noticed his depression.

'What's the matter, guy?' asked Paul during morning break.

'Aw, nothing,' said Delroy.

'Snap out of it,' said Bradman. 'If you go on like this, you gwone be dead 'fore you fifteen.'

'So what?' snapped Delroy.

'Well,' said Bradman, 'it would be sin to be dead 'fore fifteen an' never been kissed.'

'Aw, shut you mout',' snarled Delroy, and he walked off on his own, leaving his friends laughing and snapping their fingers after him.

The one good thing about Delroy's problem was that it meant he behaved himself in class all day. Not that he did any work. He was too absorbed in his own thoughts to manage that. But it meant that he wasn't distracted by his friends and didn't join in their messing about.

During lunch time, Stephen approached him.

'See you tonight,' he said. 'It's going to be a great match.'

'Sure,' said Delroy.

Did that mean he had decided to go? He didn't know. It was just his automatic reaction to Stephen's words. It didn't mean a thing.

The last lesson of the day was English. Mrs Lasky was going on about imagery. It was something about the way in which ideas were embodied in figures of speech or idioms or symbols.

'Take westerns for instance,' said Mrs Lasky. 'It's traditional for the hero to be dressed in white and the villain to be dressed in black. Why?'

Delroy couldn't think of an answer.

'Because the hero's good and the villain's bad,' suggested someone.

'But why white and black?' asked Mrs Lasky.

'Because white stands for good and black stands for bad,' suggested another pupil.

'Ah,' said Mrs Lasky. 'Exactly. Now why should people think that?'

'Because they're stupid,' explained Paul.

'Probably,' agreed Mrs Lasky, 'but that's not the answer.'

'Because it's always been like that,' said Stephen. 'Once, white people used to think they were superior so anything white was good and anything black was bad.'

'That's it,' said Mrs Lasky. 'Or something like that. And it takes a long time for people to change their ideas. These become fixed in the language and are handed down from one generation to another. Can you think of any expressions which use the word "black"?'

Delroy tried to think of some examples.

'Blackmail,' suggested someone.

'Black magic,' said another pupil.

'A black list.'

'Black market.'

'A black look.'

'That's it,' said Mrs Lasky. 'And what about the expression "to swear black is white"? Or describing someone as not being "as black as he is painted"? Or what about unions when they say they are going to "black a firm"? What kind of meaning does the word "black" have in all of those?'

'It's something bad,' said Stephen.

'Exactly,' said Mrs Lasky. 'So you see how in people's minds the notion that black equals bad goes on even if they aren't conscious of it. And since the idea is in the very language we use, it makes it all the more difficult to get rid of racial prejudice.'

'Hey, miss,' said Paul. 'That's grim.'

'Yes, I know it is. But if you are aware of it, then perhaps you can do something about it.'

'Like what?' asked Delroy.

'Like seeing through all these negative images. By creating new positive images where black stands for something good.'

'Like black is beautiful?' suggested Stephen.

'Yes,' said Mrs Lasky. 'That slogan has done a tremendous amount to raise the morale of black people.'

'Yeah,' said Paul. 'Black *is* beautiful.'

He turned to a couple of white pupils in the class. 'I

88

wouldn't want to be white like you.'

'You couldn't be if you tried,' one of them answered.

'You're just jealous because you're not black,' mocked Paul.

'No, we're not.'

'Why else do people spend all that money goin' to the Costa Brava to get a tan then?'

'Yeah, and their skin gets all burned up and peels off.'

'An' a week after they're back, they're just as pale as ever.'

This exchange of remarks made the black boys in the class throw themselves about with delight at their own witticisms. Other boys joined in the laughter. Mrs Lasky was smiling. There was no sense of tension in the air. Everyone was relaxed.

'Black people can get sunburned too,' said Mrs Lasky when the amusement had subsided.

'Can they? I didn't know that,' said Delroy.

'Anyway,' continued Mrs Lasky, 'the point is not whether white or black is better. Both white and black can be beautiful. It doesn't depend on the colour of your skin. It depends on what's inside.'

Delroy thought about what had been said. There they were again, trying to make out that everything black was bad. What chance did he stand if everyone believed that? Everywhere he went, people blamed blacks. It was in the newspapers and on television every day. Shopkeepers didn't want blacks in their shops. The police moved them on. Teachers didn't trust them. Even his father said he was bad, though Delroy wasn't really sure that that was because he was black.

He thought again about the word 'black'. He was brown, not black. But David, a white boy in the class, wasn't white either, he was pink if anything. He remembered puzzling over this before. Was there something about the word 'black' he didn't like? Could it be that he was ashamed of being called black, and that was why he preferred to think of himself as brown? He shouldn't be ashamed of it. He was what he was, and other people could think what they liked. Hadn't Mrs Lasky said, 'Black is beautiful'? She was right. Of course she was.

Delroy tried to recall what Mrs Lasky had said to him the last time she had spoken to him on his own. What was it? Something about kicking the white world in the teeth? She hadn't meant it literally. She had meant it was up to him to show that he was just as good as a white boy. Right then, he would show them. He would play in the basketball match. He would score some ranking baskets. He would help the school to beat Northlands. If his father didn't like it, hard luck. If he was locked out of his home, so much the worse. He would prove that black was beautiful.

Almost without realizing it, Delroy had made up his mind. He had found the solution to his problem.

NINETEEN

As soon as he entered the changing room, any doubts about whether or not he should have been there vanished immediately. The excitement of the other players was infectious. As they changed into their basketball kit, they joked and jeered and boasted. They were going to beat Northlands. They were going to show them what a real team was like. They were going to make them wish they had never been born.

For almost the first time that day, Delroy felt his face relaxing and broadening into a smile.

When he was ready, he bounded into the gym. The Northlands team was already there, practising and limbering up. It looked a tough team. Examining them as they warmed up, passing the ball easily to each other, or leaping up to drop the ball accurately into the basket, Delroy couldn't help thinking that they looked much older than an under fifteen team. They were so much bigger than most of the boys in his own team. It might be a good idea for Mr Miller to demand to see their birth certificates.

The other fact that straightaway struck Delroy about the Northlands team was that they were all white. In his own team, there was one white boy and one Asian. All the others were black. He couldn't understand it. Northlands school was less than ten miles away, and yet all the players were white. It was one more reason why they had to do well and beat them.

Mr Miller called the team together. They crowded round him in a circle.

'Remember what we've done in practice,' said Mr Miller. 'Set man to man. Don't let any of them get away on their own. And if they dribble, pressure them. Move backwards. Don't let them have an inch. They're taller than you are, so they've got an advantage. That means you've got to work twice as hard. Right, boys?'

The team nodded. They all felt too dry-mouthed with excitement and anticipation to be able to say anything. Mr Miller put his hand out. One after another, the boys placed their hands on top of his own. Then in unison, they cried: 'One, two, three, let's go', and they broke away.

At first, things went well. Twice Stephen was able to capture a loose ball, bounce it fast down the entire length of the gym, leap up and drop it into the basket. Then the Northlands team grew wise to this, and Stephen was heavily marked.

Delroy kept alert. He followed the action keenly, trying to intercept the ball, and marking his opposite number in the Northlands team. It was hard work. He was soon breathing heavily, and the sweat broke out on his forehead and down his back.

Gradually, the Northlands team took over. One of their players — No. 5 — had a fantastically accurate throw. Whenever he had the ball and was unmarked, he balanced himself, raised the ball in the air, and aimed it straight for the basket. Delroy stood there almost transfixed, watching the skill of it. Three times in a row No. 5 did it. Delroy began to despair. Who was supposed to be marking him?

During the break, Mr Miller emphasized this point. The boys huddled round him.

'You've got to mark your man,' he said. 'You let that No. 5 get away every time.'

'He's a good player,' said Stephen. 'He's the best on their side.'

'So what?' said Mr Miller. 'If there's someone there to pressure him, he won't be half as good. Delroy, you mark him. Stick to him all the time. Don't give him a chance.'

When the whistle went for them to resume, Delroy positioned himself shoulder to shoulder with No. 5. Whenever No. 5 got the ball, Delroy was there. Whenever No. 5 tried to dribble it down the gym, Delroy moved backwards, spreading his arms and legs wide to give his opponent as little room as possible for manoeuvre. Whenever No. 5 shot, Delroy leaped into the air to intercept or deflect the ball. Several times he was successful. He even caught the ball once, bounced it down the gym and evaded two of the opposing team before passing it to Stephen who finished off the movement by scoring a perfect basket.

'Ranking!' He heard the shout amid the applause from his own reserves sitting on the sides. He felt very pleased with himself.

Stephen patted him on the shoulder. 'Great, man,' he said.

After that, Delroy had a rest period, and sat on the side-lines watching. Whenever his own team made a good move, there were excited cheers. He was surprised at how quiet the Northlands team's supporters were. There were about half a dozen of them on the other side of the gym. They scarcely made a sound. The Northlands players too were grim and silent, concentrating on the match. They didn't waste time on congratulations or recriminations. His own friends couldn't help smiling and cheering when things were doing well, swearing and cursing when anything went wrong.

Sitting on the bench at the side of the gym, the team members commented on the game.

'When Stephen marks a man, that man's dead,' said one of them admiringly.

'Basket!' they roared as Stephen added some more points to their score.

'It was all right,' said Delroy.

'What d'you mean?' demanded Gerry. 'That was a

good basket. You wouldn't know a good basket when you saw one.'

'Neither would you,' said Delroy.

'Oh yes I would,' said Gerry.

'Why?' asked Delroy.

'I've played more games than you have.'

There was no answer to that. Delroy laughed and allowed Gerry to have his argument.

At the next rest period, Mr Miller gathered his team around him again.

'You've got to get possession,' he urged. 'Intercept more. Get the ball and then look for the gap. You've got to hustle and hustle until you get possession. That's the thing. It's a close match so far, boys. We're nearly there. It just needs that little bit more push.'

Delroy was back in the side. With renewed energy, he charged up and down the gym, keeping an eye on No. 5, seeking every chance to intercept the ball. It was nearly full time. Delroy's breath was coming fast. His legs were getting heavier and heavier. He wasn't sure how much longer he could last. He kept trying to catch sight of the score board, and at the same time concentrate on the match. When at last he managed it, he saw that the Northlands team was only one point ahead. It was now or never.

No. 5 made yet another attempt to score a basket. Delroy leaped up to deflect his throw. He missed, but the ball ricochetted off the edge of the basket and bounced out. Stephen pounced on it. He propelled it to the other end of the gym. Delroy was with him. So was the Northlands team. They were surrounded. Stephen shouted, 'Yes!' He stretched out the ball as though to pass it to Delroy. Delroy raised his arms ready to receive it. The Northlands team moved towards him. And then Stephen leaped up and dropped the ball into the basket.

It was perfect. The reserves and supporters on the sidelines went wild. They had made it. In the nick of time, they had made it.

The winners were exultant. They jumped in the air. They slapped each other on the back and let out screams of joy. Mr Miller called them back to order. They formed a

93

circle and did their 'Ra, ra, ra!' in tribute to the opposing team. Then they ran into the changing room to continue their celebration.

'Well done, Henry,' called Mr Miller. 'Well done, James. You see what happens when you get it all together. I told you, didn't I? Well done, Delroy.'

Mr Miller punched Delroy playfully in the chest. Delroy grinned from ear to ear. He was delighted with himself. He was on top of the world. He felt he could defy gravity.

The changing room was full of excited talk about the match.

'That was a close thing,' said one player.

'Rubbish,' said another. 'We made it, didn't we?'

'Great play, Delroy,' said Stephen.

'Did you see that big forward from Northlands when he had a penalty against him? He nearly punched Mr Miller.'

'You've got to psych them out,' said Gerry, 'you've got to psych them out.'

'They were so big.'

'It's tactics that work. It's strategy that counts.'

'They were so full of themselves.'

'What d'you expect from a team like that?'

'What d'you mean?'

'Well, a white team like that.'

'A white team? Yellow's more like it.'

'Watch it,' said Martin, the only white boy in the team.

'Aw, we don't mean you.'

And suddenly, Martin was surrounded by the other members of the team, patting him playfully, slapping him and roughing up his hair.

'That's all right, then,' said Martin, laughing and enjoying it. He hadn't really been annoyed. He knew they accepted him.

Delroy listened to the banter and smiled at the horse-play. He was too exhausted to join in. But it was a contented exhaustion. Half sitting, half lying on the bench, he luxuriated in the weariness that spread through his limbs.

His whole body glowed with the sense of a good job well done. It was such a satisfying feeling that Delroy was reluctant to break it by moving, by starting the effort of changing and getting into his clothes. He wanted to stay just like that for ever.

'Come on, dreamer,' said Mr Miller, touching Delroy's leg with his toe. 'I've got a home to go to even if you haven't.'

Delroy jumped up and began to get dressed. Mr Miller's words had set off a nerve. The thought of home pulsed in his head. What was he going to find there? How would his father react to Delroy turning up late? What would he do when he knew that Delroy had disobeyed him? How would Delroy be able to stand up against him?

Suddenly, the excitement and pleasure of the last hour was turned to ashes.

When he saw that his father's car was parked outside the house, Delroy feared the worst. He had half hoped that it would not be there, that he would be able to get home before his father. His mother might have let him in and covered up for him. There was no chance of that now.

Delroy put his key in the lock and turned it as quietly as possible. He pushed the door open and went in. At least it hadn't been bolted.

At the same time, the door of the front room opened. His father appeared. He confronted Delroy, his face stormy with anger.

'Where have you been?' demanded Mr Ellis. 'I thought I told you to come straight home from school.'

'I've been playing basketball,' said Delroy. He could have bitten his tongue off. His father had told him that he wasn't to play basketball any more.

'When are you going to do what you are told?' asked Mr Ellis. 'Don't say I didn't warn you.'

Delroy saw that his mother was standing in the doorway of the front room. Her eyes were wide, and one hand touched her lips.

'I'm in the school team,' said Delroy. 'They wanted me to play.'

'I don't care what the school wants,' said Mr Ellis. 'It's

what I want and what I say that matters. Are you going to do what I tell you to or not?'

Delroy felt cornered. He was damned if he could see why he should give in to his father.

'I don't see why. . . .' he began.

'You what?' yelled his father.

'I don't see why I shouldn't play basketball if I want to,' continued Delroy. 'I don't see why I shouldn't have a life of my own.'

'Not while you're living under my roof, you won't.'

'Stuff your roof,' muttered Delroy.

'What did you say?' asked Mr Ellis.

Delroy remained silent.

'What did you say?' repeated Mr Ellis menacingly. 'Come on, boy. I want to hear it.'

Delroy still didn't answer.

Mr Ellis moved towards Delroy. 'I think you need another beating,' he said.

He raised his hand. Delroy felt anger and resentment burning through him. He became rigid and still.

'Don't you touch me,' he said.

Mr Ellis's hand stayed in the air, arrested in movement. It hesitated, and then slowly fell to his side again.

'What did you say?' asked Mr Ellis incredulously.

Still very quietly, Delroy repeated his words. 'Don't you touch me. If you do, I'll hit you back.'

Father and son furiously stared at each other. It could only have been for a few seconds, but to Delroy it seemed like an eternity. It was as though time had ceased to exist. Then his father lowered his gaze. He moved back a few steps. He seemed to have grown smaller, to have shrunk somehow. But when he looked at Delroy and spoke again, his determination to dominate was as strong as ever.

'All right,' he said. 'If that's the way you want it. This is my house. If you're not going to do what I say, then you can go somewhere else. Find somewhere else to sleep.'

'But you can't,' said Mrs Ellis, coming forward.

'Shut up, woman,' snapped Mr Ellis. He pushed her back towards the front room.

He turned again to Delroy.

'So now you know where you stand,' he said. 'Either you come in and do what I tell you to, or you can get out now.'

It was his father's last word. Delroy knew that. There was no going back. Either he had to do what his father wanted, accept all the conditions he laid down, or make a life for himself. His father's pride wouldn't countenance any alternative.

Delroy found that he was shaking. His legs were like jelly. He just couldn't keep them steady. It was as though there was no bone or muscle left in them. He clenched his teeth to try to keep his body from shivering. But it was no use. He kept on shaking. He concentrated all the intensity of his hatred into the stare he directed at his father. The same intensity was returned from his father's closed face and glowering eyes. What was he to do? It was now or never.

Instantly his mind was made up. He turned and went through the still open door. He slammed it shut behind him.

TWENTY

At first, Delroy felt a great sense of release. He had finally stood up for himself. He had defied his father. He had shown that he wasn't a slave to be told what to do and to be treated like dirt under his foot. Who did he think he was, telling him what he could do? Delroy had a right to his own life, and now he was going to lead it. If his father didn't like it, too bad.

A great wave of wonder swept over him. He couldn't really believe it. His father had tried to beat him, and Delroy had dared him to do it. That had shown him. His father wouldn't attempt to do anything like that again. He would realize now that Delroy was a man. He would have to treat him like an equal in future. Delroy felt as though he was entering a new era of his life. He was smiling. He was suddenly proud and free.

Then anger returned. Find somewhere else to sleep, his father had said. It wasn't fair. Just because he had stood up to him and defied him, his father had thrown him out. It wasn't even as though he had been doing anything wrong. He had been playing basketball for the school. Any normal father would have been pleased for his son to be given such an honour. All right, then, he would find somewhere else to sleep. He didn't need his father. He would show him he could get on very well without him. He had friends, hadn't he? They would help him. He was finished with his father for ever.

Delroy hadn't really noticed where he had been going. He had been striding out, his mind lost in his thoughts and emotions. Now he found that he was near the estate where Bradman lived. That was it. He would go to Bradman's. He would help him. Bradman's flat was always full of people. There were his brothers and his brothers' girlfriends who seemed to change every week. There were cousins and uncles who dropped in and dossed down between jobs or between houses. There were always beds and people sleeping everywhere. There would be room for Delroy.

He passed a crowd of children playing ball in the concrete squares between the tower blocks. Other children were chasing and teasing each other. In the darkness, their voices bounced back from the sheer walls of the flats as though magnified in an echo-chamber.

The lifts were still not working, and the lights were still out of action. Delroy groped his way up the staircase. When he knocked at the door of Bradman's flat, it was opened by his brother, Errol.

'Bradman not 'ere,' said Errol. ''E gone out.'

Delroy's first reaction was one of dismay. He could hear laughter and raised voices from behind Errol's back.

'Come on in,' said Errol. 'Come join us. Plenty rum.'

Errol's voice dissolved in a high-pitched giggle. It sounded strange coming from such a thick body.

'Or beer,' he went on. 'You prefer beer?'

Delroy didn't answer. Instead, he asked, 'Where's Bradman gone?'

'I don' know, man,' replied Errol. 'You know Bradman. 'E could be just 'bout anywheres. You go ask the law. They probably does know where Bradman.'

'I'll try the Paradise,' said Delroy.

'You do that, little boy,' said Errol. 'An' you tell that Bradman when he does get 'ome, the father does plan to give 'im a whole 'eap o' lashes.' Again, Errol's voice broke into a shrill giggle.

A second figure emerged from the room inside. It was Phil, another of Bradman's brothers.

'Does you know where Bradman?' Errol asked him. ''Is little friend want to know.'

''E gone by Franklyn yard,' said Phil. ''E 'elpin' wit' one o' 'is gigs. 'E won' be back tonight.'

An irritated voice called from within the room.

'I comin',' shouted Errol, and he shut the door.

Delroy was disappointed. He had expected it to be so easy. He had thought that all he had to do was call on Bradman. Bradman would welcome him in. He would be able to spend the night there. Now this plan had fallen down. There was no point in trying the Paradise. He didn't know where Franklyn lived. And even if he did, he couldn't go there.

Emerging again at ground level, Delroy was conscious that it was getting cold. There was a frosty chill in the air, and his breath came out in clouds of steam. He snuggled deeper inside his anorak and plunged his hands in his pockets.

He was also feeling hungry and tired. His stomach was very empty, but he didn't have any money to buy food. He couldn't decide whether his tiredness was due to the basketball match or to his hunger.

He pulled himself together. This wouldn't do. He would have to put up with his rumbling stomach and aching limbs. Bradman wasn't in, and there was nothing he could do about it. But Bradman wasn't the only friend he had in the world. There were others. He could try them.

He took stock of where he was. If he went back the way he had come, he would pass Ant'ny's house. Ant'ny would help him.

Ant'ny lived above a television shop in one of the

shopping parades. The entrance to the flat was a narrow door at the side of the shop. Delroy couldn't see a bell to press, so he knocked. While waiting for someone to answer, he stepped into the roadway and looked up. The lights were on upstairs. There was someone in. He hoped that Ant'ny was there. Bradman had let him down by being out. It would be too much if Ant'ny did the same.

As he moved back to the door, it opened, and Ant'ny appeared.

'Hi, man,' said Ant'ny. 'What you doin'?'

'I've been turned out,' explained Delroy.

'You mean your dad's thrown you out?'

'Yes.'

'Oh no, man,' said Ant'ny. 'That's grim. What you gwone do?'

'I thought you might be able to help,' said Delroy.

'Sure, man, sure,' said Ant'ny.

There was a call from above. Delroy looked up the steep flight of stairs behind Ant'ny. It must be his mother.

'Ant'ny,' came the voice, deep and loud and insistent. 'Who that, Ant'ny?'

'Oh, hell,' said Ant'ny. 'That my mum.'

'So what?' said Delroy.

'She don' like friends callin'.'

'But what am I gwone do?' asked Delroy, growing concerned. 'Can't you do anything?'

'I'd like to 'elp,' said Ant'ny. 'You know I would. But my mum won' let me. There's not'in' I can do.'

'Ant'ny,' came the demanding voice again from upstairs. 'What keepin' you?'

'Look,' said Ant'ny. 'I've gotta go. She'll be mad if she find out.'

'But what am I gwone do?' repeated Delroy, nearing despair.

'What 'bout Paul?' suggested Ant'ny. 'Perhaps 'e can 'elp.'

A shadow, a large shadow, appeared at the top of the stairs. Ant'ny looked apprehensively over his shoulder.

'I've gotta go,' he whispered urgently. 'Try Paul.'

And the door was shut in Delroy's face.

He stood there wondering what to do next. Inside, he could hear Ant'ny's mum loudly demanding who had been at the door, and Ant'ny replying, 'It wasn't nobody, Mum. Honest.' Then he turned away.

He thought bitterly about his friend. Ant'ny was always the first to stand up for his rights, always the first to protest and say you shouldn't let anyone do you down. Then when it came to the crunch, what happened? He was too scared of his mum to do anything. A fat lot of good he was as a friend.

Some stories about Ant'ny came back to him. Hadn't there been talk of him being sent back to Jamaica? Ant'ny had got into some trouble at school, and his mother had said that if there was any more she would send him back to Jamaica. Jamaica? It didn't mean any more to Ant'ny than it did to Delroy. Just like Delroy, Ant'ny had been born in Britain. He had never been to Jamaica. Still, Delroy knew that the threat had been very real. It was a threat that many of this friends' mothers had made. No wonder Ant'ny was careful to do what his mother told him to.

Delroy looked about him. It was getting late. He cursed the fact that his watch didn't work. He only wore it for show. He didn't know what the time was. But then he realized that it didn't matter. It seemed hours since he had defied his father and stormed out of the house. But it couldn't be. It was certainly hours since he had last had something to eat. He remembered that day's school lunch — spam, coleslaw, beetroot, a roll, and a slab of sponge cake with some icing on top. At the time, he had shovelled it away without thinking about it — except to complain as he always complained, and as all the other boys did. Now, he would have given anything to be sitting down to have it all over again.

He began to walk without really knowing where he was going. He passed a pub. The sound of loud voices came from it. A car had just drawn up. A group of people tumbled out of it. One of them bumped into Delroy. He was pushed out of the way. For a moment, anger spurted up inside him. But by the time he had decided to do something about it, the people had vanished inside the pub.

Further on, he passed a grocer's shop still open. Looking through the window, he saw that it was an Asian shop. The hunger inside him grew deeper. He could see displays of biscuits, cakes and crisps. There were sweets and chocolate and nuts. No one was in the shop except the owner who was sitting at the till going through his accounts. Delroy had no money. It would have been impossible to try to steal something with no other customers there. He moved on.

A sex shop still had its lights on. Delroy stopped to stare at the magazines in the window. The covers showed girls in all kinds of positions thrusting themselves forward to the viewer. They were bursting out of their clothes. Delroy had seen magazines like these before. His friends sometimes brought them to school and flashed them in front of each other at break. They giggled over them and hurriedly put them away whenever a teacher came in sight.

The doorbell jangled, and Delroy gave a guilty start. A large black man came out. He studied Delroy, and his face broke into a grin. He gave Delroy a nudge and pushed him away.

'You too young, man,' he said. 'Too young.'

Again, anger burst up in Delroy. He practically snarled at the man before turning and walking away.

Too young, too young! That's what they all said. His father treated him like a baby, expecting him to obey his rules and do what he was told. He was a man. He could lead his own life. He would show them yet.

What had Ant'ny said? He had suggested Paul might be able to help. Delroy wasn't going to give in that easily.

Delroy had been to Paul's before. But it had always been during the day, and he had usually been with other friends. Now, at night, as he walked down Paul's street, he wasn't sure which house it was. He thought it was about halfway along, but he couldn't remember the number. He stopped outside No. 20, looking for some identifying sign. He was almost certain it was either No. 20 or 22. But which?

In the small front garden of No. 22 was a large pyramid

102

of sand. A great pile of broken lathes was heaped untidily on top of one another in the corner, and a heavy old-fashioned sink lay abandoned on its side. Paul's father was a do-it-yourself fanatic. Paul was always complaining about the mess he had to live in as his father tackled one improvement after another. This must be the house.

Delroy pressed the bell and waited. It seemed to be getting colder. Perhaps he was just feeling hungrier. Paul would find him something to eat.

Nobody came to the door. For a desperate moment, Delroy feared there might be no one at home. Then what would he do? He pushed the thought away. There was a light on in the hall. There must be someone in. He pressed the bell again.

This time he heard the clatter of feet approaching. The door opened. It was Paul.

'Hi,' said Paul, his usual cheery self. 'Come on in.'

The stairs and hall were uncarpeted. The walls had been stripped of paper. They were patched here and there with polyfilla so that they had a mottled effect. The smell of plaster and paint was everywhere.

Paul led the way into the kitchen. There, huddled round the television set, were Paul's mother and his two younger sisters. They looked like refugees sheltering from the storm.

'There ain't nowhere else,' explained Paul as though apologizing for the chaos.

At that moment came the sound of hammering from upstairs. Paul's mother raised her eyes to the ceiling, her face completely devoid of expression. Then they returned to gaze vacantly at the television screen. She completely ignored Delroy — she probably wasn't even aware that he was in the room.

He and Paul sat at the kitchen table and exchanged conversation in conspiratorial whispers.

'How are things, man?' asked Paul.

'Not so good,' said Delroy. 'My dad's thrown me out.'

'What 'appened?' asked Paul.

'We had a row,' explained Delroy.

He didn't need to say more than that. Paul understood.

103

'That's dread,' said Paul.

He cast a nervous look at his mother, but she was absorbed in her own sorrows.

'What you gwone do?' Paul asked.

'I don't know,' said Delroy. 'I thought you might be able to help.'

'Well, I'd like to,' said Paul, 'but I don' know 'ow. The whole 'ouse is upside down.'

'I thought you could put me up for the night,' said Delroy, pressing his need.

'I'd like to 'elp,' said Paul, sincerely. 'The trouble is that Dad's got 'is decoratin' craze again. 'E's goin' right through the 'ouse. 'E's mad. Most normal men would do one room at a time. But 'im? Oh, no. 'E t'inks it's better to strip all the wallpaper first right through, an' then do all the paintin', an' then do all the wallpaperin'. The result is that none o' the rooms is fit to live in. This is the only one 'e 'asn't touched so far.'

'It doesn't matter,' said Delroy, getting desperate. 'I can sleep anywhere.'

'Yes, but I don' know where,' said Paul.

'You put Gerry up when he was thrown out.'

Delroy remembered hearing how Gerry had been smuggled up to Paul's bedroom after his parents had turned in for the night, and how he had been smuggled out again before they got up in the morning.

'Yes, but I 'ad my own bedroom then,' said Paul. 'I'm 'avin' to sleep in the same room as those two'— he pointed to his sisters — 'until this mess is finished wit'. An' I can tell you that's no joke.'

Delroy saw his hopes evaporating. Already, he was back in the cold dark streets with nowhere to go.

'You might be able to sleep in the front room,' said Paul cautiously. 'There's a sofa in there, so at least you could stretch out.'

'That's great,' said Delroy, cheering up.

'It's covered in dust sheets,' said Paul. 'That could be quite useful. If someone comes in, you can 'ide under them. You could even pretend you're a ghost.'

They suddenly found this was funny and collapsed

104

into a fit of giggling. When they emerged, they found Paul's two sisters staring at them solemnly. They subsided.

'I'll make a show of lettin' you out,' said Paul, 'an' then you can go into the front room. You can leave in the mornin' before anyone's up.'

'Thanks, Paul,' said Delroy. 'That's perfect.'

Delroy's other pressing need burst to the surface again.

'Have you any food?' he asked. 'I haven't eaten anything since school dinner.'

'I'll see what I can do,' said Paul. He sounded doubtful.

He stood up. Making sure that his mother and sisters were still glued to the television set, he crept stealthily to the dresser beside the fridge and took down a large Quality Street sweet-tin. He held it in the crook of his arm and began slowly to ease the lid off.

Delroy watched him anxiously. The lid was tight, but it was moving. The saliva of anticipation started to gather in his mouth, and he swallowed. A quick look told him that Paul's mother and sisters hadn't noticed anything.

Then there was a sudden clatter as the lid shot off and out of Paul's hand. The tin fell with a crash to the floor.

Paul's mother was up from her seat and beside the dresser with a speed that took Delroy by surprise. She was yelling loudly and cuffing Paul. His sisters glared at him aghast.

'Now look what you done,' she shouted. 'Didn' I say you was to leave that cake alone?'

She stooped down and scooped the cake and crumbs from the floor back into the tin. She recovered the lid, snapped it firmly on, and put the tin back on the dresser, on the top shelf this time. Paul had retreated to his seat next to Delroy again. He raised his hands to protect his head as his mother aimed a final blow at him.

'You'll be the death o' me,' she went on. 'You an' the father. My nerves is all shot to bits. I'm ill, that's what I am. I don' know what I done to deserve this. The Good Lord know I never done not'in' to deserve all this.'

Gradually, her moaning subsided. She sat down. Her eyes returned to the television screen and glazed over. The two girls settled in their seats again. There was silence in the room except for the droning voice coming from the set.

Paul and Delroy sank back into gloom. Delroy's stomach would just have to go on rumbling.

'Sorry,' whispered Paul at last.

'Don't worry,' sighed Delroy. 'At least you tried. And you've got me somewhere to sleep.'

'Yeah,' said Paul, cheering up. 'That's somethin'. We'd better do it now.'

He pushed his chair back.

'Delroy's goin' now,' he announced.

''Bye, Delroy,' said Paul's mother. Her glazed eyes didn't leave the television set.

Paul's sisters looked at Delroy with their huge eyes, but they didn't say anything.

Paul opened the front door, and said for the benefit of anyone who might have been listening, 'See you tomorrow, Delroy. Thanks for callin'.'

He then shut the door, and the two boys crept quietly into the front room. Paul closed the door and switched the light on. The furniture had all been placed in the middle of the room and was covered by a series of white dust sheets. Paul pulled one off.

'That's the sofa,' he whispered. 'It should be all right.'

Delroy nodded.

'I'll leave you then,' said Paul.

At that moment, the door burst open. Paul's father appeared. He was dressed in splashed and stained overalls with turned-up bottoms. He wore a flat cap on his head. His face and beard were daubed with paint. He was carrying a gallon tin of emulsion and a large paint brush. There was a demoniac gleam in his eye.

'What you doin' 'ere?' he demanded. 'Out. I gwone finish this room tonight.'

'But Dad — ' began Paul.

'Out,' repeated his father.

Paul and Delroy looked at each other. There was nothing they could do about it.

'Sorry,' said Paul.

He let Delroy out the front door.

'Well, you tried,' said Delroy again, and he stepped into the road. The door was shut behind him.

Delroy felt as though the end of his world had come. Everything had gone wrong. If only the cake tin hadn't been so awkward. If only Paul's father hadn't come in at that very moment.

He huddled inside his anorak, stuffed his hands in his pockets, and set off. What was he to do now? There were other friends, but he didn't know them that well, and he wasn't certain where they lived. Anyway, it was getting late, and he couldn't guarantee what kind of welcome he would get. He felt depressed. Everything seemed to be against him. It was as if it had all been planned to make things as difficult as possible for him.

It wasn't fair. Adults like his father held all the cards. There seemed to be no way in which he could get away from them and lead his own life. Still, he was damned if he was going to give in. He would rather walk the streets all night than admit defeat.

He hadn't been paying much attention to where he was going. He had been walking aimlessly. Now he looked around him. The shops and houses had petered out. On his right was an open space. It was the park not far from his home. He decided it was as good a place as any even if it was dark. A path cut through the park linking one part of the district with another.

As he walked along he realized again that he was tired. He wondered how much longer he could go on. It was time he had a rest. There was a bench beside the path. He would sit down there and try to sort things out.

A surprising number of people went by on the path, taking a short cut home, even at this time of night. They emerged out of darkness into the arc of light thrown by the street lamp near the bench and vanished again into darkness. Delroy didn't pay them much attention. He watched them in an abstracted way as part of the visual horizon, but his thoughts were far away.

What exactly had his father said? He had been taken aback by Delroy's defiance. He had spoken in anger. Perhaps he hadn't meant what he had said. Perhaps he would think differently when he had calmed down. Delroy's storming out might even have given him something of a shock. He might even be worried about where Delroy was. Perhaps he was regretting his angry words.

Delroy's thoughts were interrupted by someone sitting down on the bench beside him. He glanced curiously at his neighbour. It was a white man, quite old by Delroy's standards. The odd thing was that Delroy had an impression that he had seen the man before. He had a vague recollection that the man had already walked up and down the path several times before sitting down. Delroy hurriedly looked away.

'It's getting chilly, isn't it?' the man said suddenly.

Delroy turned to examine him. The man was smiling. It was quite a pleasant smile, friendly and open. Delroy grunted agreement. He could feel the cold seeping through his anorak.

'What are you doing out on your own?' the man asked.

Again, Delroy looked at the man's face. What business was it of his? He could be out on his own if he wanted to. He wasn't a child. He could take care of himself. But the man seemed to be genuinely interested and concerned. For a moment Delroy wondered whether he should tell him about his problems. It might be a relief. The man might be able to help.

But then Delroy decided against it. Nobody could help him. 'Nothing,' he said in answer to the man's question. 'Just passing the time.'

He was aware out of the corner of his eye of the man becoming restless. He kept looking up and down the path as though to make sure there was no one about. Then he turned his attention to Delroy again. He put his arm along the back of the bench and moved a little closer.

'Why don't you come back to my place?' he suggested. 'It's nice and warm there.'

Delroy was taken by surprise. He hadn't expected this. A certain grim amusement ran through him. He had been searching for shelter from his friends all night without success, and here was a total stranger offering it to him. He turned to study the man again. He seemed all right. And

108

yet there was something that made Delroy feel suspicious.

'No,' he said, adding, 'thanks.'

'Come on,' coaxed the man, touching him lightly on the arm. 'We could have a drink of coffee or something and get warm. It's not far from here, just the other side of the park. We could be there in five minutes.'

Delroy didn't say anything. He was weighing up the situation. The way the man put it, it sounded tempting — a warm place, a drink of coffee, perhaps some food. His stomach grew as hollow as a cave at the thought of it. But then there was the man. He didn't know Delroy. He could be anybody. Why was he doing this?

The man stood up. 'Coming?' he asked encouragingly.

Delroy found himself on his feet.

'That's right,' the man said. 'It won't take us long to get there.'

As they walked through the park, the man talked and asked questions — what was his name, how old was he, which school did he go to, did he like sport, what kind of music did he listen to, and so on. Delroy answered briefly at first, but gradually he began to relax. He was pleased that someone was taking an interest in him.

The man was right. It took only five minutes to reach the place. It was in a small block of flats facing on to the park. He led the way through the main entrance to a door on the ground floor, unlocked it, and held it open for Delroy to go in.

The lights in the entrance hall were already on, and Delroy wondered if there were other people there. He could feel the warmth as soon as he entered. The central heating must have been turned up very high. The lights were on in the living room as well, three or four of them in different parts of the room casting pools of light which gave a gentle, golden glow. The room was small, but from a quick glance Delroy saw that it was very clean and tidy. He had the impression somehow that everything was expensive. The curtains and the sofa were velvet. The carpet was thick.

The man helped him off with his anorak and laid it across one of the armchairs.

'You can take your sweater off as well if you like, when you get a bit warmer,' he said. 'Sit yourself down.'

He gestured towards the sofa, and Delroy slowly lowered himself on to it. The man came and sat beside him. He put his hand casually on Delroy's knee.

'Now what would you like?' he asked. 'Coffee? Or would you like something stronger? Beer? Whisky?'

Delroy wasn't sure. He had never drunk whisky.

'Perhaps we'd better play safe and have coffee,' the man said. He patted Delroy's knee and stood up. 'I'll only be a minute.'

When he had gone out, Delroy relaxed. It was certainly comfortable here. The glow from the table lamps was soft on the eyes. The touch of velvet under his hand as he stroked the pile rough and then smooth was a soothing sensation. The warmth of the room after the cold outside eased through his body. The man was right. He would soon have to take off his sweater. He felt his eyes closing and jerked them open again. If he wasn't careful, he would be asleep in a moment.

After his failure with his friends he had been lucky to end up here. This was better than any of their houses. How long would he be able to stay, though, he wondered. The man wouldn't let him stay all night, would he? That would be too much to expect. And yet the man had been kind. If he explained what had happened, the man might let him stay. He could spend the night quite comfortably curled up on the sofa. It was worth trying.

At that point the man returned, carrying two large cups of coffee. He put them on the low table in front of the sofa and sat down beside Delroy again. The coffee was hot. Delroy took a couple of sips. The steam made his face sweat, and the liquid burned inside his chest. He became tense again, wondering how he could lead round to asking if he could stay the night.

And then he was blurting it all out, about the row with his father, about his attempts to get help from his friends, about not knowing what to do next. The man listened sympathetically. He made noises of concern. He patted Delroy on the back to comfort him.

'Of course you can stay the night,' he said. 'There's no problem about that.'

Delroy sensed an immense relief. He could hardly believe it. Everything was going to be all right. He was going to have shelter for the night, a place to sleep. He would show his father that he didn't need him, that he could look after himself. His difficulties might start again tomorrow, but he would deal with them when they arrived. For tonight, he was safe.

He turned to the man and gave an embarrassed but heart-felt smile. 'Thanks,' he mumbled.

The man was sitting on the sofa at an angle facing Delroy. His elbow was on the back of the sofa and he was resting his head on his hand and gazing at Delroy.

'You're a good-looking boy,' the man said admiringly, 'or young man, rather. You've got a good body. I can see you play a lot of sport.'

Delroy didn't know what to reply.

The man placed his hand on Delroy's thigh and pressed it. 'Good solid legs,' he said. He left his hand there.

Delroy stared at the white hand against his blue jeans. He felt the heaviness and the warmth of it.

Suddenly he realized why the man was being so kind, letting him into his home, giving him a place to sleep — what the man was after. He had heard about such things. The sweat on his face turned cold. His chest was pounding. The man's hand was still on his thigh.

A great terror filled Delroy. He had to get away. But he was frozen. He couldn't move. Then a spurt of anger rolled up inside him. Who did this man think he was? He just wanted to use him like all white men wanted to use him. Well, he wasn't going to let him. His anger had released him. He found he could move. He stood up, bumping the table and making the coffee spill into the saucers.

The man had snatched his hand away and was leaning back. His smile had gone and he was looking guarded and apprehensive.

Delroy controlled himself. 'I'm going,' he said.

The man was standing now, too. 'There's no need,' he said. 'I can help you.'

111

He stretched out his hand as though to take Delroy's arm, but Delroy shrugged away. He stumbled across the room to pick up his anorak.

'It's not like that at all,' the man was saying, his face screwed up with what looked like despair. 'I want to help you.'

But Delroy didn't wait to hear any more. He had to get away before his anger exploded. He pulled on the front door and nearly kicked it when it wouldn't open. Then he turned the Yale knob, and the way was free. He swung the door back behind him, leaving it gaping wide. He didn't bother to look round to find out whether the man was there.

Once in the dark street again, he made for the park. His anger gave him energy, and he strode fiercely along. He thought bitterly about his unfinished coffee, about the food and the bed that might have been. If only things had turned out differently. He might have known it was too good to be true. What else could he expect?

In the park, Delroy slowed down and looked about him. It was deserted now. It must be really late. He suddenly felt let down and alone. What was he going to do? How was he going to get through the night?

The thought of home flooded his mind. He licked his lips nervously. It wasn't far away. He started moving again. His feet were leading him in that direction before his brain had even decided.

It was worth one more try. A few minutes' brisk walking brought him to the front door of his house. At last, he was home. It was amazing how quickly he could move once his mind was made up. His tiredness seemed to have gone. He didn't feel cold any more. It was as though a heavy burden had been lifted from his shoulders.

Even so, he paused on the doorstep and hesitated. He couldn't prevent a sharp tug of fear from pulling at his stomach as he thought of the scene ahead. He gritted his teeth. He would have to face it. He would have to take whatever was coming.

His key was in his hand. He put it into the lock and turned it. But even before he pushed the door to try to open it, he knew that it was bolted on the inside.

TWENTY-ONE

He couldn't believe it. They had locked him out. At first, he stared at the door, numb and confused. Then a towering anger broke within him. He felt like hammering the door down with his bare fists. He wanted to wake the whole street with his fury and frustration. Everyone ought to know how inhuman his parents were to turn him out and abandon him.

Then Delroy's anger hardened into resolution. Right, he thought. If that's the way they wanted it, he would show them. He didn't care. He would manage without them. He would never go back — never again. That was the end of it.

He thrust his way on to the street again, slamming the gate behind him. But underneath the grim determination that tensed the features of his face and protected him from the chill air was a hollowness.

All evening, as he had gone round his friends desperately seeking shelter, he had never really believed that his father would actually lock him out. What Delroy had been doing was asserting his independence. He had been showing his father that he didn't need him, that he could organize his own life. Always at the back of his mind there had been the feeling that if things went wrong, his home was waiting for him, his father would take him back. It just needed the right word, like a password in a fairy tale, for everything to be restored to normal.

Now no magic formula, no Open Sesame, would unbolt the door. Now the safety net had been snatched away, and Delroy would have to venture on the tight-rope without it.

It had all been a great show of bravado. But it hadn't worked out. And now his father had called his bluff. His father had won.

Suddenly, Delroy was shivering again. A wave of fear swept through his body. What was he to do?

113

The streets Delroy was walking through were well known to him. He had often been out here at night before. But then he had been with his friends or had been going somewhere. There had been an aim in view. Now he was alone. He had nowhere to go. The streets and buildings, the garish lights and patches of darkness, pressed in upon him. They seemed strange and unfamiliar.

He searched his mind and tried to remember what had happened to his friends when they had been afraid to go home or had been locked out. What had they done? How had they managed? Sometimes, friends had put them up, but Delroy had tried that without success. Others had slept in garden sheds or derelict houses or disused factories. Perhaps he could try to find one of those. He couldn't just go on walking.

Then he remembered the bus garage. That was a possibility. Someone — was it Clinton? — had used a bus as a sleeping place for the night. He wasn't far from the garage now. It was worth a try. What alternative was there?

There were still a few people in the streets — noisy groups rolling home from parties or clubs, or single figures hurrying to the warmth of home and bed from work in hospitals or London Transport. Nobody gave Delroy a second look, and he didn't take much interest in them.

Then he saw ahead of him two shapes which made his eyes widen. They were policemen. They were walking towards him. Some instinct told him to get out of sight. He retraced his steps hurriedly and turned off the main street. He hid himself in the shadow of a doorway.

As he waited for the policemen to come into view at the end of the street, a host of memories came flooding back to him about police harassment of his friends. They had been picked up for no reason at all. They had been charged with breach of the peace or insulting behaviour or obstructing the highway. They had been charged with 'sus'. The police could invent anything if they wanted to and make it stick.

At last the policemen passed the end of the road. Delroy pressed himself against the doorway. He followed them with his eyes as they crossed the road and vanished beyond the next block of shops. He waited to make sure they were well away before he emerged and resumed his walking.

Delroy was now near the bus garage. He knew it well. It was where he usually went in the morning to get his bus for school. It wasn't far from where he lived. In the mornings it was a busy place. Bus crews would be arriving and clocking on. Inspectors were bustling about looking important, calling for buses to get off on schedule. There was the revving of engines and the scream of whistles as buses manoeuvred for position before hurtling out into the tide of traffic.

Now, as he came within sight of it, all seemed quiet. The great barn of the garage was silent, but not deserted. There were floodlights on, and there were still people about — all-night mechanics seeing to repairs, or cleaners sweeping buses out ready for their morning runs. There were buses everywhere, filling the garage itself and spilling over into the forecourt.

Delroy didn't know what to do. He couldn't remember the details his friends had told him, but the buses in the forecourt seemed the best bet. At least they were in the open. If there were any problems, he could make a quick get-away.

He looked up and down the street. There was no traffic passing. As far as he could see, there were no pedestrians. He raced across the road. The first bus would be too obvious and too dangerous. He slipped along to the third in line. It was only then that he realized that something was wrong. The automatic shutters at the entrances and exits of the buses were closed. Delroy clawed at them in an attempt to pull them open but only succeeded in breaking a finger nail. He knew they could only be operated from the driver's cabin.

Delroy was becoming desperate. Why hadn't he thought of this before? How long ago had it been since he had heard of one of his friends sleeping on a bus? It was almost as though a new type of bus had been introduced to prevent that kind of thing from happening.

There must be some of the older type of bus there — the

115

kind with the open entrance at the back where you jumped on. Delroy squeezed in between the lines of buses, feeling his way along their sides. It wasn't too long before he found what he was searching for, and his panic was over. With a final look about him, he stepped on to the boarding platform and slipped up the stairs.

The back seat was the best place. At least there he would be able to stretch out, and he would be near the exit if any danger should threaten.

He tried it for size. He couldn't lie full-length. He had to lie with his knees bent forward. He buried his head in his arms to provide a kind of pillow. Already his eyes were closed. The weariness of the day was overcoming him. Instantly, he was aware that it was cold. He pulled the hood of his anorak further down over his head. Uncomfortable though he was, he felt himself sinking into sleep. He screwed up his face so that his eyes burrowed deeper and deeper into his eyelids.

The outside world was unimportant What did it matter if his mother and father had locked him out? He was too tired to think about them. He was too tired even to remember how hungry he was. Sleep was all that mattered.

TWENTY-TWO

Delroy was awakened by the cold. Although the orange glare from the floodlights filtered into the bus, he could tell that it was still night outside. There was frost on the window. Delroy shivered. He disentangled himself to look at his watch to find out the time, and then remembered that his watch wasn't working. For all he knew, it could still be hours before morning.

He heard a voice shouting jocularly in the distance. Could it be an all-night mechanic or someone arriving for the morning shift? He was suddenly alert, and sat upright, discovering that his body was stiff and aching. He looked through a piece of the window that had not frosted over. There were figures walking about — more than he had

116

noticed a few hours earlier. The day must be beginning even if the skies were still dark.

His feet and legs were numb. He rubbed them to try to get some life back into them. It was cold. Only by an effort of will was he able to stop himself from shivering. The desire to lie down and go back to sleep was strong, but he resisted it. He would have to get moving.

But before he could put his will into action, he was aware that the sounds of activity were growing louder. They seemed to be in the very bus itself. He could feel the bodywork shake as though someone very heavy had boarded it. There was the sound of clumsy footsteps shuffling up the stairs. Delroy huddled on the seat, making himself as small as possible.

It was a cleaner. She had arrived at the top of the stairs, puffing and out of breath, and was making her way to the front of the bus. She was a broad, squat figure, wearing overalls, and wrapped in a huge woollen cardigan many sizes too big for her. Delroy moved his head forward so that he could watch her ambling progress up the bus. Then with a lunge, he was off the seat and making for the stairs. As he scuttled down, he looked back and was conscious of a shriek, a startled, white face and a dropped brush. But he didn't care about that. All that mattered was getting off the bus and out of the garage. He was surprised at how quickly his stiff muscles responded to the urge of necessity.

Jumping off the bus he didn't bother to check whether there was anyone about or not. He didn't care who saw him so long as he got out of that place. He charged down the line of buses, careering against the bodywork and bouncing from side to side in his haste. It was like being a ball on a pin-table. At last he found a way free and reached the street. Then he ran.

It was only when his breath was coming short and fierce that he slowed down and stopped to take stock of his position. Now what was he going to do? He didn't know what time it was. Five o'clock? Six o'clock? When did the bus service start? Anyway, it was early, and he had hours to fill before school began.

He stumbled along the road, shaking his head to prevent his eyes from gluing up. His mouth was dry, and the thought of a hot drink or of breakfast made his stomach turn over. None of the shops he passed was open. It was too early for that. In any case, his pockets were empty.

Delroy had no idea how he was going to spend the next hours. Was there somewhere else he could hide? Somewhere else he could sleep until the world began again and it was safe to come out into the open? He remembered the policemen he had hidden from the night before. The streets were deserted at this hour, and he was certain to look a suspicious character to any policeman who passed.

Still he blundered on aimlessly, going where his feet took him. Gradually, figures appeared as the day began and people set off for work. Whenever he saw someone approaching him, he hunched himself up and his steps took on a more purposeful manner as though he had some definite objective in mind. But really his mind was a blank. He didn't know where he was going. The only thought at the back of his head was that school began at nine o'clock, and at least there he would be able to see Bradman and his other friends. They might be able to give him some advice on what to do next.

By now Delroy had left the shops and was walking down a residential street. Ahead of him he saw a milk-float and heard the wheeze and jangle as it set off, stopping and starting as the milkman proceeded with his deliveries. An idea came into Delroy's mind. Here was a possibility.

He studied the milkman's comings and goings as he moved slowly up the street delivering his milk. Delroy crossed to the other side of the road. The milk-cart moved ahead of him and then stopped. Delroy drew level. The milkman jumped from his cabin. He took four bottles from a crate and turned away from the float.

Immediately Delroy leaped across the road. He seized a bottle from one of the crates and pushed it inside his anorak. He had a fleeting glimpse of the milkman walking up the path towards the door of a house. As he retraced his steps to the other side of the road, his trainers made no sound on the tarmac. Then he walked on, resisting the

118

temptation to look behind him. He heard the whine as the milk-float was put into operation again, but he walked fast. The noise of the engine and the rattle of milk bottles were soon far behind.

He left the road at the next turning. He passed a number of houses until he came to one with a garage, furthest away from the street lighting. In the doorway of the garage, he took the milk bottle out of his anorak. Forcing the top off, he put the bottle to his lips and drank. The milk was cold, just as it was when he took it from the fridge at home, but it tasted even better. Between gulps, Delroy looked at the top which he still held in his hand. It was a gold top. That was a bit of luck. Delroy felt like smiling for the first time that morning.

By the time he had drunk the last dregs in the bottle, his stomach was full and bloated. That was better. He was ready now to face the day. A dog had appeared on the other side of the road. It was a thin, bedraggled specimen of indeterminate breed — not the kind that was pampered at home and had a warm bed for the night. It was sniffing more in hope than in expectation at the gate-post of the house opposite.

On an impulse, before he could stop himself, Delroy threw the milk bottle at the dog. It fell short, on the edge of the pavement, and shattered into many pieces with a loud report. The dog jumped into the air and fled, its ears pressed low against its head and its tail drooping. It was almost comic. Delroy laughed out loud at the suddenness with which the creature took to its heels and the terror with which it scuttled away.

At the same time, he realized what a fool he had been. He leaped from the garage doorway into the road and raced in the opposite direction from the dog.

'Rass,' he swore to himself. 'You idiot. You've woken up the whole street,' and he went on running.

But again he couldn't prevent himself from laughing. Audible chuckles burst from his lips. There was suddenly an exhilaration in running past the rows of houses still dead to the world, their occupants smothered in sleep. Delroy felt like shouting. He felt like waking the whole world to tell them that he had survived, that he wasn't afraid of being on his own, that he could look after himself. He didn't need anyone else to help him. The stiffness and the cold of a few hours ago were forgotten in his new-found confidence.

Without realizing it, the words of his favourite reggae song were on his lips.

'Africa — a — a,'
he began to sing,
'Africa, the Zion land, oh
That the place I long to be, oh
That the place I long to be.'
He fitted his steps to the rhythm of the tune.

Delroy turned the corner, and fell straight into the arms of a policeman.

There were two of them. Their hands gripped him firmly. Their white, blotchy faces were grimly fixed upon him.

'Where are you running to?' demanded the larger and older of the two policemen.

Delroy's excitement evaporated. It was as though the breath had been knocked out of his body. He felt the strong fingers biting into the flesh and muscle of his arms. He sensed the suspicion and hostility steaming from the policemen's eyes. Any attempt at escape, and they wouldn't hesitate to break his arms. All the fury of a trapped animal rose up inside Delroy, but he knew better than to try to escape.

'I'm not running anywhere,' he mumbled, trying to keep the anger that glowered in his eyes out of his voice.

'Listen to that,' said the second policeman mockingly. He was younger and more athletically built. 'When did you ever see one of these blackies running if he didn't have a good reason for it?'

Delroy reared in resentment at these words, but the hands simply held him more firmly. He was no match for the policemen. They were much bigger and stronger than he was.

'He's got a bit of spirit at any rate,' said the first policeman.

'Yes, a damn sight too much if you ask me,' said his companion. 'These blacks think they own the place.'

Again, Delroy heaved in protest at this insult. The grip on his arms became piercing and painful. The policemen studied him with wary eyes and tightened faces.

'I think we'd better search him,' said the second policeman, pretending to be jocular. 'See what he's got.'

Delroy was suddenly spun round and thrust face-forwards against the wall. His nose hit the brickwork, and the sharp pain made tears spring to his eyes. His arms were spread wide above his head. The palms of his hands were ground into the rough grittiness of the surface. His legs were jerked violently apart so that he almost fell. Hands moved down his back, along his hips and down the outside of his legs. Then the hands moved up again between his legs. They groped round to feel his pockets and up over his chest.

Delroy felt tears of humiliation and shame join those of pain. He was so helpless. They could do anything to him. He clenched his teeth, determined that the tears would not flow.

'He's clean,' said the first policeman.

'That's a pity,' said the other. He sounded disappointed. 'Shall we book him?'

'What for?'

'We could book him on sus. After all, he was running when we found him. There might have been a break-in, or we might walk round the corner and find somebody with his face kicked in. Perhaps he's just mugged an old woman. You never know. It's just the kind of thing this sort gets up to.'

They were talking about him as though he wasn't there, as though he was a block of wood which couldn't possibly have any feelings. His arms raised up against the wall were growing tired. He wanted to examine his nose to see what damage had been done.

'It would serve him right,' went on the younger policeman, 'if we took him down to the station — give him a real fright.'

'What's the point?' asked the first policeman. 'It just

121

means more paper work. It's not worth it. We can take his particulars in case something turns up.'

'You mean let him go?'

'Yes. Come on. I'm getting cold standing here.'

There was a pause, and then Delroy heard the younger policeman say, 'All right, Sambo, you can turn round.'

He had taken out a notebook. Delroy rubbed his arms and stared at him sullenly.

'What's your name?' the policeman demanded.

Delroy gave it.

'Can't you even speak English?' asked the policeman in disgust. 'Say it again.'

Delroy repeated his name.

'I can't make out a word you're saying. You come and live in this country, and you can't even speak English. Say it properly.'

Delroy held his breath desperately for a moment and glared at his questioner. The older policeman had lost interest and had wandered off to the corner of the street. He was looking up and down.

For the third time, Delroy gave his name, as loudly and clearly as he could.

'That's better,' said the policeman. 'You're beginning to learn. Address?'

Delroy gave it.

The policeman sighed with mock patience. 'That's no good. We're back where we started. I can't understand that. Why can't you speak properly? Try it again.'

Delroy repeated his address.

'There you are. You see? You can speak proper English when you try. What school do you go to?'

Delroy named his school.

'Oh, I might have known. A right lot of black thugs they've got up there. It's a real training ground for the detention centre.'

The policeman flipped his notebook shut. He put his face close to Delroy's and spoke quietly and confidentially. The pores in his white skin and the hairs in his nostrils were visible as though through a magnifying mirror. Delroy bowed his head with an appearance of

122

submissiveness.

'Look, Sambo,' the policeman said. 'I'll give you some advice. If you want to live in this country, you've got to behave yourself. Not that anyone wants you here. Because they don't. If we could get rid of you tomorrow just like that, then we would. And we're going to be watching you all the time. You put one step out of line, and we're going to get you. Understand?'

Delroy didn't trust himself to reply. He kept his head lowered, avoiding contact with those hard, hostile eyes. The policeman moved away, and Delroy heard the slap of his boots on the pavement. When he eventually looked up, the policeman was joining his companion at the end of the street.

'I don't think we'll have any more trouble with that one,' he was saying.

Delroy felt weak and shaken. The tears which he had been restraining for so long threatened now to burst in torrents over the rims of his eyes. He screwed up his face and held them back. Even though there was no one to see, he wouldn't give the police that satisfaction.

'The bastards,' he muttered between teeth clenched together to keep them from trembling and to grind out his hatred.

He took a deep breath. He wiped his eyes with the sleeve of his anorak to mop up any tears that might have escaped. Then he pushed himself off the wall and walked slowly back to the main road. The policemen had disappeared. There was no one else in sight.

Without thinking, Delroy turned to the right. It didn't matter which way he went. His feet carried him mechanically along while his mind grappled with bitter thoughts.

He brooded over the policemen and the way they had treated him. Perhaps he should make an official complaint against them. But what was the point? He didn't know their names or numbers. Anyway, who would believe him? No one would take his word against that of a policeman. He knew boys who had made complaints against police behaviour, but none of them had ever been successful. There was no way you could win against the police.

That didn't stop indignation and anger from swelling up inside him. They had no right to treat him like that. But where did right come into it? People could do what they liked with him. He had no rights. If he had been white, they wouldn't have treated him like that — humiliating and insulting him in the way they had done.

And yet, from what his friends had said, he had got off lightly. He had heard stories of boys being punched and kicked, being bodily lifted up by the arms and legs like sacks and thrown into police vans, being kept in a police cell without a charge for hours. He had got off lightly compared with them.

All that talk about speaking English. He had been treated like some ignorant foreigner. He had been born in England. As far as he was concerned, he was as English as anybody. He was black, but so what? He had as much right to be English as anyone else — if only other people would let him.

He remembered his previous encounter with the police in the shopping centre when they had taken his name and address. Would there be some sort of tie-up? Would they feed his name and address into a computer, and would the machine go ping when it came up with the fact that it already had the information? Would the police go round to his home and question him further? Would they fudge up some phoney charge to get him into trouble? There was no telling what they would do.

The thought of home came rushing back to him. What did it matter if they did go there to persecute him further? They wouldn't find him there. He didn't have a home any longer.

TWENTY-THREE

There was no danger that Delroy would be late for school that morning. There was nowhere else for him to go. With no money in his pockets, there was no point in stopping off to buy some biscuits or crisps. Nor did he fancy the idea of stealing any. After his encounter with the police, he thought it advisable to be careful. The only possibility of breakfast was cadging it off his friends.

When Delroy reached the playground he was horrified to see that it was almost deserted. He had never been at school as early as this, not even when he managed to make it for pre-school basketball practice. Usually, it was a case of a mad rush up the drive as the bell was ringing to arrive at school before the prefects started taking the names of late-comers.

There were one or two figures sitting disconsolately on the benches round the playground, or half-heartedly kicking a tennis ball about the asphalt. None of his particular friends had yet turned up.

Delroy saw his hopes of breakfast receding. His friends wouldn't be there until nine o'clock. If then. Often they rolled up quarter of an hour late. Delroy wondered how long he could endure the pain of hunger in his stomach, and the dry, dirty taste in his mouth. If he were at home he would be able to brush his teeth and rinse out his mouth. At about this time, he would normally be sitting down to his breakfast — cornflakes, bacon and egg, toast, coffee. His stomach ached even more at the thought of it.

He noticed Stephen arriving. Stephen was always in good time for school.

'Hey, man,' greeted Stephen, 'that was a great match last night.'

'Sure,' replied Delroy, 'ranking,' though his voice didn't betray much enthusiasm. He had forgotten all about the basketball match. Had it really taken place only the evening before? It seemed an eternity away. Delroy felt as though he had lived a whole lifetime of events since then.

'You're early,' said Stephen.

At first, Delroy suspected he was being got at. But Stephen's tone was one of neutral fact and his face was innocent. In any case, Stephen wasn't the kind of person to make sneering remarks.

Delroy looked at Stephen's broad, open face speculatively. Stephen was sensible and intelligent. His advice would be worth having.

125

'I didn't go home last night,' Delroy said.

'What d'you mean?' asked Stephen.

'I was locked out.'

'Where did you sleep then?'

'At the bus garage.'

'That sounds a bit rough,' said Stephen sympathetically.

'I didn't know where else to go,' went on Delroy in a burst, relieved to be telling his story to someone. 'I tried some friends, but they were no use. Then I remembered Clinton and how he had spent the night on a bus, so I tried that. And then. . . .'

Delroy stopped suddenly. He didn't want to tell Stephen about the police.

'Why were you locked out?' asked Stephen.

'Because of the match. My dad said I was to come straight home from school and not play basketball.'

'That's too much,' said Stephen, very concerned. And then he went on to ask the question which had been nagging below the surface of Delroy's mind all morning as he had been walking the streets. 'What are you going to do tonight?'

'I don't know.' And he didn't. The future was a blank. He couldn't bear to think about what he would do if he had to spend another night away from home.

'You'll have to make it up,' said Stephen.

'How d'you mean?' asked Delroy.

'You'll have to say you're sorry and do what your dad tells you to.'

'I can't do that,' said Delroy indignantly.

'Why not?'

'He's the one who's in the wrong.'

'That's got nothing to do with it,' said Stephen. 'If you want to survive, you sometimes have to make allowances. You can't expect to go on having your own way all the time.'

Delroy didn't like the advice he was getting. The fact that he knew that what Stephen said was right didn't help. That was the trouble with Stephen. He was always right.

'It's all very well for you,' said Delroy. 'You don't have

problems with your parents.'

'That's what you think,' said Stephen grimly. 'Just because I don't talk about it don't mean I've no problems. I just put up with them, that's all. I know they won't last forever. One of these days I'll be able to lead my own life. And it's going to be the best kind of life I can make it.'

Delroy couldn't think that far ahead. He had to get through the coming night first. He walked away, feeling suddenly depressed and tired. Stephen would make it. There was no doubt about that. But what about him? Would he be able to make something of his life? He practically had a police record already. Then there were his parents. Supposing he took Stephen's advice. Supposing he went back home and his parents wouldn't have him? What would he do then? The thought was too grim for him to bear.

When the bell for the start of school rang, Delroy hurried to the top of the drive to await the arrival of his friends. And there they were as usual, barging up in a rush.

'Have you something to eat?' Delroy demanded. 'I'm starving.'

'Why, man?' asked Bradman. 'Get up too late for breakfast?'

'No,' said Delroy. 'I ain't been home.'

'Yeah, 'ow did you get on?' asked Ant'ny.

They crowded round him, and Delroy told his story.

'Now you know what it's like, man,' said Bradman, and left it at that.

The pangs of hunger returned.

'Have you anything to eat?' Delroy demanded again with increased urgency.

'Sure,' said Bradman. 'What would you like? Crushed flies or custard creams?'

'Custard creams,' chose Delroy. They were his favourites.

'Just as well,' said Bradman. ''Cos that's the only kin' I've got.'

He took a packet of biscuits out of his shoulder bag and opened it. Delroy knew better than to ask his friend where he had got the biscuits.

127

When Delroy had eaten four of the custard creams, stuffing them into his mouth whole, Bradman yelled, 'Hey, leave some for after.'

He took the packet back and put it in his bag again.

'What you gwone do tonight?' Bradman asked.

'I don't know,' said Delroy. 'I'll have to think about it.'

'Don' you go 'ome,' urged Ant'ny. 'That'll teach 'em a lesson.'

Delroy nearly laughed in his face. Who was Ant'ny to give advice like that? He remembered with bitterness his friend's scared face the night before when his mother had called him. Ant'ny wouldn't dare do anything to cross his mother, and here he was telling him to go on defying his parents.

'I've got some money,' said Bradman. 'That might 'elp.'

At that moment, Mr Brown, who was on duty, came storming across the playground towards them.

'What are you boys hanging around for?' he demanded. 'You should be in your form rooms by now.'

The boys pretended to ignore him.

'I'll see you about it at break,' said Bradman.

'All right,' said Delroy. 'Thanks.'

And having calmly concluded their conversation, the boys went their separate ways to their classrooms, leaving Mr Brown glaring angrily after them.

The first lesson of the day for Delroy was maths. He didn't have his maths book. He didn't have any books. He knew as soon as he entered the classroom that there was going to be trouble.

When the clatter of chairs and the gossip had subsided, and the last late-comers had arrived, Mr Trencher yelled, 'All books out, on the desk. Have them ready so that I can see. I want all books out.'

This was a familiar routine with Mr Trencher. Delroy knew that he only had to wait — wait for Mr Trencher to see his bare desk for him to rant and rave at him. Here he was now.

'Where is your book, Ellis?' Mr Trencher asked.

'I haven't got it,' replied Delroy. It was useless to explain that he hadn't been home the night before and therefore hadn't been able to get his maths book.

'Out you go then,' said Mr Trencher. 'You know the rule in this classroom. You might get away with it with other teachers, but not with me. If you can't be bothered to bring your book, you don't get a lesson.'

'But,' began Delroy, having second thoughts. Perhaps Mr Trencher would listen.

The teacher hadn't even heard him.

'It's always the same,' Mr Trencher went on. 'I don't know why I bother to try to teach. You treat this place like a social club. You just come here to chat with your friends. The fact that this is an educational establishment seems to have escaped your notice. The idea never even enters your heads.'

Delroy gave up. Even if he had explained, Mr Trencher wouldn't have heard him.

'I told you to get out,' said Mr Trencher, looking at Delroy with indignant surprise at the fact that he hadn't yet moved. 'You can spend the period outside the door. You don't deserve to be educated.'

'Rass,' muttered Delroy between his teeth as he got up.

'What's that?' asked Mr Trencher.

'Nothing,' said Delroy wearily. He made his way to the door.

'Now then,' said Mr Trencher to the class, 'perhaps we can get on with the lesson.'

Delroy went out of the classroom and closed the door. Standing outside the class was always a bore. There were always teachers passing up and down, and most of them gave you dirty looks. Sometimes the nice teachers would stop and speak to you and show some concern. Mrs Lasky, if she passed, would put her arm round him or punch him in the chest and say playfully, 'I could murder you!' and he would grin and look ashamed, and yet know that she didn't think any the worse of him for being put out.

He hadn't said anything to Mrs Lasky at registration that morning about being turned out of the house. It had crossed his mind that she might be able to help. He knew she would want to help. Whether she would be of any use or not was another matter. She might be able to 'phone his mother up. It would be one way out of the difficulty.

Delroy looked through the window in the door at the lesson. He was annoyed at missing maths. He liked the subject. He was good at it. Although Mr Trencher was a bit hard, he was a good teacher. If only he had been more understanding. It wasn't Delroy's fault that he didn't have his book with him.

He was still hungry. He felt and heard his stomach rumble. In spite of the biscuits Bradman had given him, there was a great void down there that needed to be filled. He might be able to get some more biscuits from Bradman at break to see him through.

He was suddenly awakened from his thoughts by a shout.

'Get away from that door.'

He looked up to see Mr Frobisher advancing on him.

'Mr Trencher doesn't want you peeping in on him and interrupting his lesson,' Mr Frobisher said.

'I wasn't doing anything,' said Delroy sullenly.

'That's what you say,' said Mr Frobisher. 'Why are you standing out here anyway?'

'I didn't have my book,' explained Delroy, 'so Mr Trencher told me to wait out here.'

'Isn't that just typical?' said Mr Frobisher. 'You never do have your books.'

'Yes, I do,' retorted Delroy becoming loud and angry. 'It's not my fault I haven't got my maths book.'

'Oh, tell me another one,' sneered Mr Frobisher. 'You're the perfect student, I suppose.'

'No, I'm not. But I'm not as bad as you say either. I can't do any good with you around.'

'So now it's all my fault, is it?' said Mr Frobisher.

Delroy felt himself growing hot all over. Who did Mr Frobisher think he was, speaking to him like that? His whole body stiffened and became tense. His fists clenched. He could hardly move his lips.

'Who do you think you are?' he forced out between his teeth.

Mr Frobisher raised his eyebrows. He looked mock-ingly at Delroy.

'I know who I am,' he said. 'I very much doubt though whether you know who you are. You certainly don't know the kind of behaviour expected in a civilized place.'

Delroy's breath deepened. He licked his lips and searched for an answer.

'I — I — ' he began.

Before he could go any further, he was interrupted by the arrival of the headmaster.

'Ah, there you are, Delroy,' said Mr Johnson. 'I was looking for you.'

'He's been thrown out of another lesson,' pointed out Mr Frobisher unnecessarily.

'Yes, so I see,' said Mr Johnson, remaining calm, 'but that's not what I want to see him about. Come along, Delroy, I want to have a little talk.'

Mr Johnson took Delroy's arm and moved him in the direction of his office. Mr Frobisher was left fuming.

In his room, the headmaster told Delroy to sit down and pulled up another chair close beside him.

Delroy felt weary and battered. Mr Frobisher's sneers and accusations on top of everything else were more than he could bear. He felt as though his guts were being churned up inside him. He felt as if his face had been whipped raw, as though he had spent hours battling against a driving wind. Now here was the headmaster. There were going to be more problems.

'I've just had a 'phone call from your mother,' said Mr Johnson. 'She's very worried about you.'

Delroy looked at the headmaster, his eyes wide and round. This was not what he had been expecting. A flicker of hope flared up inside him, but it was short-lived. He noted that it was his mother who had 'phoned up, not his father. And in any case, it was rather late for his mother to become worried. Where was her concern last night? A mood of desolate bitterness overwhelmed him.

'You weren't home last night,' Mr Johnson went on, 'and your mother's very anxious about where you were.'

'What does she care?' mumbled Delroy resentfully.

'Of course she cares.'

'Why did she bolt the door then?' challenged Delroy.

'You mean you were shut out?'

'Yes.'

'Where did you go?'

'I just walked about.'

Delroy could sense Mr Johnson looking at him and hesitating, but he avoided glancing at the headmaster and stared steadfastly at his hands which lay lifeless along his thighs.

'You see, Delroy,' said Mr Johnson slowly, 'people say and do things sometimes which they don't necessarily mean. All right, the door was locked on you last night, but if your mother really didn't care, would she bother to 'phone this morning to find out if you are in school and what happened to you?'

Delroy didn't know. He was confused. He couldn't think straight anymore. Mr Johnson was always trying to persuade and convince you with his logic, but at the moment, Delroy couldn't sort it all out.

'She also said the police had been round,' continued Mr Johnson.

At this, Delroy shot the headmaster a quick, guilty glance, and then looked hurriedly away. That was something he had feared but hadn't really believed would happen.

'What's it all about, Delroy?' asked Mr Johnson gently.

'Nothing,' said Delroy.

'Come on,' coaxed the headmaster. 'We may be able to help.'

Delroy hesitated and then said, 'I got stopped by the police this morning. They wanted to know what I was doing.'

'And had you been doing anything?' asked Mr Johnson.

'No, I hadn't,' said Delroy indignantly.

'All right, all right,' said Mr Johnson reassuringly. 'I believe you.'

He patted Delroy on the shoulder to calm him down.

Then he stood up.

'Wait outside, will you, Delroy?' he said. 'Your mum's at home. She's taken the morning off work. I'll give her a ring and tell her you're all right. Then we'll try to work out the best thing to do.'

Alone once more, Delroy began to feel a little glow of cheerfulness returning. Perhaps it was going to be all right after all. The fact that he had stayed out all night might have given his parents a shock — at least his mother. The police coming round would also get them worried, though Delroy guessed they'd have a few things to say to him about that. He was coming round to the view that what Stephen had suggested was possibly the best solution. He would do what his father said. It was better than walking the streets all night or sleeping in the bus garage.

He could go home now and see his mother and talk it over. Mr Johnson had said she was there. If he could get some money for his bus fare, he would get home all the more quickly. Bradman had offered to lend him some money at break. But Delroy couldn't wait till then. If he could find Bradman, he could get the money now.

He set off along the corridor to the nearest classroom and looked in. It was a second-year class. He tried the next classroom.

'Are you at it again?' demanded a voice.

Delroy turned and saw Mr Frobisher.

'I've told you already this morning not to look in at classes and disturb lessons.'

Delroy felt his body stiffen as his hope and his self-control slipped away. It was just too much.

'Get away from that door,' roared Mr Frobisher.

He put his hand out and pushed Delroy.

'Don't you touch me,' snarled Delroy. 'Get your filthy hands off me.'

Delroy's vision became blurred. Who was this figure standing in front of him? Who was this person with the white face telling him what to do, pushing him out of the way? It was time he got off his back.

'Don't you talk to me like that,' said Mr Frobisher.

Who was this person, this teacher, this policeman,

this father, ordering him about? Why didn't he speak to him like a human being, instead of treating him like a dog or a bit of dirt?

'I'm not going to be spoken to like that,' went on Mr Frobisher.

Delroy saw himself do it. He saw himself lift his arm and bring it down on the side of Mr Frobisher's neck. He saw Mr Frobisher's mouth open wide in amazement. He saw Mr Frobisher fall to the ground against the wall. His eyes were staring upwards in fear.

Mr Johnson was there. Mrs Lasky was there. Mr Johnson was helping Mr Frobisher to his feet. Delroy heard Mrs Lasky asking, 'What happened?' He felt Mr Johnson holding him, pulling him away.

Then he was in Mr Johnson's office again. There were voices outside. Mrs Lasky was speaking angrily. 'You fool,' she was shouting, 'I've put hours into that boy to try to get him through, and you destroy it all in a minute. What the hell have you been trained for? What the hell are you being paid for?' Then she was suddenly silent.

Mr Johnson came in and closed the door.

Delroy's senses returned to him sharp and clear. The fog had lifted. He was appalled. He was now fully aware of the enormity of what he had done. It was something which couldn't be brushed aside or forgotten.

He watched the headmaster walk across the room and slump into the seat behind his desk. Mr Johnson covered his face with his hands and sat there for a few moments without moving. Delroy gazed at him anxiously. The headmaster slowly parted his hands, and his face was revealed. His eyes stared steadily at Delroy. There was absolute silence in the room. At last, the headmaster spoke.

'You've really done it this time, haven't you, Delroy?' he said.

Delroy could make no reply. What could he say? He knew that the headmaster's statement was true. He lowered his eyes.

'I had hoped,' went on the headmaster, 'that we would be able to get you through, give you enough support

to carry you over a bad patch, but it hasn't been possible —
for one reason or another.'

He moved some papers aimlessly about his desk.

'You know what it means, don't you, Delroy?'

'Yes, sir,' said Delroy.

He wasn't sure. But it was bound to be something
serious.

'I'm sorry it has to end this way, but I can't see any
alternative. You'd better go home now.'

'Yes, sir.'

'Tell your mum and dad I'll be writing to them.'

'Yes, sir.'

Delroy got up.

'Goodbye, Delroy.'

'Goodbye, sir.'

Delroy left the office.

TWENTY-FOUR

Delroy had to walk home. He hadn't seen Bradman to
borrow his bus fare from him. He was more tired and
hungry than ever. He walked along like an automaton,
scarcely aware of his feet touching the pavement. But
although his body was numb, his mind was frantically
active. There was so much to think about.

The vision of Mr Frobisher lying on the floor, his
mouth open, his eyes wide with fear, haunted him. He
grew angry. He didn't regret what he had done. Mr
Frobisher deserved everything that had happened to him.
If he were in a similar position again he would do exactly
the same. Mr Frobisher had asked for it. He had been
asking for it for a long time. If Delroy hadn't hit him,
someone else would have done. Who did Mr Frobisher
think he was, treating him like dirt? Nobody deserved to be
spoken to the way Mr Frobisher spoke to black pupils at
that school. Perhaps he spoke to all pupils the same way.
Delroy wasn't sure. All he knew was that Mr Frobisher
treated black pupils as though they were inferiors or

slaves, and no one was so perfect that they could behave like that. Delroy was glad he had knocked him down.

And yet, at the same time, there were doubts. He knew he shouldn't have done it. No one, no matter how unpleasant he was, deserved to have that happen to him. After all, Mr Frobisher presumably thought he was doing his job going around yelling at pupils and bossing them about. There might even be some pupils who liked him, though Delroy found that difficult to believe. Oh, why did it have to happen? Why wasn't it possible to go back an hour and start again? But it was too late for that now. The deed was done, and he would have to face the consequences.

What would they be? He would probably be expelled or transferred to another school. He knew he couldn't hit a teacher and get away with it. The school would have to do something about it. He couldn't go back there. Mr Frobisher might even take him to court. He had every right to do so. Even Delroy saw that. Mr Frobisher had asked for it, but Delroy still shouldn't have hit him.

If he went to a new school, it would mean leaving behind the teachers who had helped him and whom he had grown to like over the past three-and-a-half years. He was sorry he hadn't seen Mrs Lasky before he left. She had been good to him. He had felt that she had always been on his side. She had understood him and tried to help him. There was also Mr Miller. He had always regarded Delroy as a human being. He had always behaved towards him with respect. And Mr Johnson was all right, too. He was soft, but at least he had tried. He was all right.

It would mean leaving his friends as well — Bradman, Ant'ny, Paul and the others. He could imagine them at break gathering together and talking about the latest event.

'Where's Delroy?'
'What 'appened?'
''As he been suspended?'
'Mr Frobisher? Oh, no! I don' believe it!'
'You get expelled for that.'
'That's grim, man.'

136

'Mr Frobisher got what 'e deserved.'

'Still, it's 'ard luck on Delroy.'

Oh well, thought Delroy, what did it matter? He could still go on seeing his friends outside school, and he could always make new ones.

A picture of his future school began to form itself in Delroy's mind. Perhaps it wouldn't be too bad. It would be a fresh start for him, a second chance. He could begin again and keep out of trouble and show the kind of person he really was. Then the shadow of Mr Frobisher fell across his thoughts again. There would be Mr Frobishers at his new school. How would he face them? Would he attack them as well? Perhaps he wouldn't be allowed to begin a clean sheet and show the real him.

He wasn't even sure who the real him was. Mr Frobisher had taunted him with not knowing who he was. He wasn't certain what Mr Frobisher had meant. But he was definitely confused. Some people like Mrs Lasky saw good in him. Others like Mr Frobisher and his father called him a bad boy. The police had no hesitation in recognizing him as a villain as soon as they saw him.

He wanted to be good, but other people wouldn't always let him. No, that wasn't altogether true. He had to straighten himself out. He was so mixed up. Stephen had no difficulty in being good regardless of what other people did. Bradman made no pretence of trying to be good. Which of them should Delroy be like? If only he could get it all together, as Mr Miller kept saying.

And then there were his parents. He had deliberately been putting off thinking about them. But eventually he could no longer prevent thoughts of them from seeping through and dominating his mind. He was on his way home. It wasn't far now. What was awaiting him there? What kind of reception would he receive?

If only there were no one there. He would wash his face, clean his teeth, have something to eat, and go straight to bed. That would be lovely — to lose himself in sleep and wake up to find it had all been a dream.

But there would be someone there. His mother was waiting for him. Would she be full of questions? Would she be concerned and want to know how he had spent the night and how he had managed? Or would she be cold and reproachful?

The police had been round. She wouldn't like that. Should he tell her how they had treated him? Would it matter to her?

And then there was the business at school to explain. How would his mother take this new development, this new shame that he was bringing on the family? Would there be more rows? Would he be thrown out again? Delroy just didn't know what to expect.

Perhaps he could win her round. Perhaps he could play on her feelings for him. Mr Johnson had said that she was worried about him. But then there would be his father to face as well when he came home from work. He wouldn't be won over by having his sympathies played on. He had said he was never going up to the school again over Delroy, and as far as he was concerned Delroy was no longer a son of his. Delroy's expulsion would simply be another blow to his pride, another reason for him to reject his son.

The nearer he approached home, the less certain Delroy felt. It was all so bewildering. It was like trying to disentangle a mass of muddled string when you couldn't find the beginning or the end. Only one thing was definite. A decision of some kind about his future was going to be made. And it was going to be made soon. It couldn't be put off. It was going to be made now.

Delroy had reached home. He stood on the doorstep for a moment, pulling himself together and gathering up his courage. He blew his breath out a couple of times in short hard bursts like an athlete before a race. Then he rang the bell to warn his mother that he was there and put his key in the lock. He turned the key and opened the door. His father was standing there facing him.

Panic seized Delroy. He couldn't move or say anything. He hadn't expected his father to be home. He hadn't noticed his car parked outside. He hadn't bothered to look. Now, he stood transfixed, staring at his father, wondering what was going to happen.

In turn, his father was staring at him. His face was

blank and impassive. Delroy couldn't tell what kind of mood he was in. Then his father spoke.

'Come in, Delroy. Don't just stand there. Your mother's waiting.'

The tone was impatient but not unkind. Still, Delroy hesitated. He didn't move.

'It's all right,' said his father. 'We know what happened at school.'

Mr Johnson must have 'phoned. His father knew about Mr Frobisher. And his father wasn't angry. He wasn't fuming and yelling and threatening. Delroy couldn't believe it. He kept waiting for the blow to land.

And when his father stepped towards him, Delroy thought the blow was coming. He tensed himself to receive it. But instead, Mr Ellis put his hand on Delroy's arm.

Delroy felt the pressure. It was firm but reassuring. He looked down at the hand. It was strong and brown. No, it was black. It was black and beautiful. The grip tightened, and Delroy allowed himself to be drawn into the house.